"He's a real white hat," he heard her brother whisper behind him. *"Isn't he?"*

Sloan didn't wait to hear Abby's answer as he let himself out through the front door. Whatever the white hats were that the kid was talking about, Sloan knew that he'd never worn one.

Abby might be the first woman he'd felt any interest for in a long while.

But white hats were for the good guys.

They weren't for the guys who'd only ever hurt the ones who least deserved it.

* * *

RETURN TO THE DOUBLE C: Under the big blue Wyoming sky, this family discovers true love

D0037074

Dear Reader,

What occurs between two people when "that moment" hits? When they realize that *this* is the person they want to be with from here on out? Can it be linked to one specific moment? Or does it develop slowly, over time? Or is it all of that and something more?

For Abby and Sloan, that moment hits quickly. She's not surprised, and he's not ready. But he gets there and she's waiting when he does.

How about you? Do you believe in love at first sight? Tell me about it at Allison@allisonleigh.com. I'd love to hear your stories. And if you'd like, I'll share with you the recipe for Abby's chocolate cookies. Because you never know...it may be the way to someone's heart!

All my best,

Allison

A Weaver Beginning

Allison Leigh

HHARLEQUIN® SPECIAL EDITION®

Recycling programs
for this product may
not exist in your area.

ISBN-13: 978-0-373-65770-4

A WEAVER BEGINNING

HARLEQUIN®
www.Harlequin.com

Printed in U.S.A.

Books by Allison Leigh

Harlequin Special Edition

Silhouette Special Edition

Other books by this author
available in ebook format.

ALLISON LEIGH

There is a saying that you can never be too rich or too thin. Allison doesn't believe that, but she does believe that you can *never* have enough books! When her stories find a way into the hearts—and bookshelves—of others, Allison says she feels she's done something right. Making her home in Arizona with her husband, she enjoys hearing from her readers at Allison@allisonleigh.com or P.O. Box 40772, Mesa, AZ 85274-0772.

For Greg.

Chapter One

The snow covered everything.

Everything except the clear strip down the middle of the street that had been plowed just that morning.

Looking out the front window of the house he'd been renting for the past six months, Sloan McCray studied that strip.

While the middle of the street was whistle clean, the displaced snow formed two-foot walls against the curb on both sides of the street, blocking driveways and parking spaces.

Generally speaking, Sloan didn't worry about the snowplow job as long as it was done. It was his first winter in Weaver—the first snow had fallen in October and hadn't stopped since. He'd had two months to get used to it.

There were five houses on his street. Some of the folks occupying the homes had snowblowers—ancient ones kept running by ingenuity and stubbornness, and new ones that cost as much as Sloan's first motorcycle. He dealt with the annoying snow berm in front of his house the old-fashioned way—with a heavy-duty snow shovel and a lot of muscle.

Not a problem for him.

He'd been well used to being physically active, even before he'd signed on as a deputy sheriff here in Weaver. Pitching heavy snow out of his driveway was a welcome task.

Kept the muscles working.

Kept the mind occupied with the simple and mundane.

Two good things, as far as he was concerned.

He wasn't sold on living in Weaver yet. His job was temporary; he had a one-year lease on the house. He needed to start thinking about what to do after the nine months he'd promised Max Scalise—the sheriff—were up. He should have been spending less time with the snow shovel and more time thinking about what the hell he was going to do with the rest of his life. But tackling that particular question was no more appealing than it ever was.

Standing inside the warmth of his living room, Sloan eyed the snow blocking the driveways. The small blue car had been sitting on the street in front of the house next door for nearly an hour. Footsteps in the snow trailed back and forth from the car to the house.

New neighbors. Moving in on the last day of the year.

He'd been watching them for a while. The woman was young, with shining brown hair that bounced around the shoulders of her red coat with every step. The little kid with her had the same dark hair.

He'd also noticed there wasn't a man in the picture. Not to help them unpack, anyway. Nor to clear away the snow blocking the driveway, much less shovel a path to the door.

He turned away from the window, grabbed his down

vest and headed out the back of his house to the small shed where he stored his bike and tools.

It was the last day of the year and he'd spent too much time thinking already.

Time to start shoveling instead.

"Abby. *Abby*."

Balancing the heavy box in her hands, Abby Marcum glanced at her little brother. He was clutching the plastic bin containing his collection of video games against his chest, his wary gaze glued to the tall man striding toward them from the house next door. "Who's that *man?*" Dillon was whispering, but his nervousness shouted loud and clear.

"I don't know," she said calmly. "We'll meet lots of new people here in Weaver."

"I don't want new people." His pale face was pinched. "I want our old people."

She hid a sigh behind a smile. Her seven-year-old brother wasn't the only one with misgivings about moving to Weaver. But she wasn't going to show hers to him when he already had more than enough for them both. "We still have our old people," she assured him. "Braden's not so far away that we won't visit." Just not every day. Not anymore.

She hid another sigh at the thought.

Noticing that the man angling across the deep snow had nearly reached them, she looked at Dillon. "Take your box inside. You can think about where to put the television."

He clutched the bin even closer as he retraced his path from the car to the house, not taking his wary attention away from the man for a second.

Abby adjusted her grip on the packing box. She hoped that moving to Weaver hadn't been a huge mistake. Dillon had already endured so much. For two years, she'd tried to follow her grandfather's wishes. He was gone, but she was still trying. She just didn't know if moving Dillon away from the only place of stability he'd ever known had been the right thing to do or not.

The sound of crunching snow ceased when the man stopped a few yards away. "You're the new nurse over at the elementary school." His voice was deep. More matter-of-fact than welcoming.

She tightened her grip on the heavy box, trying not to stare too hard at him. Lines radiated from his dark brown eyes. His overlong brown hair was liberally flecked with grays. What should have been pretty normal features for a man who looked to be in his late thirties, but the sum of the parts made him ruthlessly attractive.

She'd grown up in Braden, which was the closest town of any size to Weaver. She knew how small-town grapevines worked, so she wasn't particularly surprised that he knew about her before she so much as opened her mouth. "I am. But I'll be splitting my time with the junior high." The schools were next door to each other, sharing their facilities. "I'm Abby Marcum." She smiled. "And you are…?"

"From next door." He stabbed the shovel into the snow.

She'd assumed that, given that he'd *come* from the house next door. "So that answers *where*." The muscles in her arms were starting to shake, so she started toward the house, her boots plowing fresh paths through the snow. "What about *who?*"

"That looks too heavy for you."

"Does it?" She kept right on moving, passing him on her way toward the three steps that led up to the front door.

"Would have been easier if you'd cleared the driveway before you started unpacking."

Her fingers dug into the cardboard. "Probably," she agreed blithely and lifted her boot, cautiously feeling for the first porch step. She'd have needed a snow shovel for that, though, and that wasn't something she'd bothered trying to cram into her small car along with everything else. Weaver had hardware stores, after all. And neighbors who had shovels to borrow, too.

The man gave a mighty sigh, his bare hands brushing hers as he lifted the box out of her grasp. "The bottom's about to give way," he said and walked past her into the house.

She hurried after him. "Um, thanks." He was already setting the box on the narrow breakfast bar separating the small living room from the even smaller kitchen. One look at the cardboard told her he was right. The crystal inside could have crashed right through. She flipped open the box and pulled out a few of the glasses she'd wrapped so carefully in newspaper just to make certain they'd safely survived. "My grandmother's crystal."

"Mmm." He didn't sound particularly interested as he looked around the living room. She'd bought the house furnished. And while the furniture that occupied the room was dated, it was clean and in good condition. With the half-dozen boxes that they'd already carried in stacked on the floor against the wall next to the brick fireplace, the small room was almost full. "It's freezing in here."

"I know. Something's wrong with the furnace. I'll get a fire started, though, soon as I get the car emptied. And once the holiday is over, I'll call someone in to get the furnace going."

She smiled across at Dillon, who was perched nervously on the edge of the couch, watching them with big eyes. He still wore his coat. She'd bought it at a clearance sale last year expecting that he would have grown into it by now. But he still looked dwarfed in it. "A fire will have us toasty warm in no time," she told her little brother brightly.

"And then we get popcorn like you promised?"

Dillon loved popcorn like almost nothing else. "Absolutely."

"You've got wood?"

At the deep-voiced question, she focused on the man and felt something jolt inside her. *Lordy.* He really *was* handsome. And vaguely familiar. "Um…no. No wood. But I'll get some." Along with that snow shovel. Having one of her own was better than borrowing.

"Stores are closed today and tomorrow for New Year's." His voice was even. Unemotional. "I've got plenty, though. I'll bring some over." He turned on his boot heel and left the house.

"Who *is* he?" Dillon whispered once he was gone.

"The neighbor. You can put away your games in the television cabinet. Soon as I finish with everything, I'll play a game of 'White Hats 3' with you." She'd gotten the latest version of the video game for him for Christmas and it was already his favorite. "Okay?"

He nodded and she went back outside.

The man had left the snow shovel sticking out of the snow banked against the side of the porch. She looked from it to the house next door. It was two-storied and twice the size of hers.

Definitely large enough to hold a wife and kids if Tall-Dark-and-Nameless had any.

She trudged back to the car and pulled the box containing their new television from the backseat. Her girlfriends from Braden had pooled their money together to buy it as a going-away present. It was mercifully lightweight, and she was heading up the steps with it in her arms when the neighbor appeared again bearing a load of wood in his arms.

She quickly got out of his way as he carried it inside.

He crouched next to the brick hearth and started stacking the wood. As he worked, he looked over at her brother. "What's your name?"

Dillon shot Abby a nervous look. "Dillon."

The man's face finally showed a little warmth. He smiled slightly. Gently. And even though it was directed at her little brother, Abby still felt the effect.

She let out a careful breath and set the television on the floor. Her girlfriends had also given her a box of Godiva chocolates before she'd left, with instructions to indulge herself on New Year's Eve—and share the chocolates with a male other than her little brother.

The chocolates were in her suitcase. She could give the box to her no-name neighbor and technically live up to the promise she'd made. Of course, he'd probably take the chocolates home to his wife. Which wasn't exactly what her girlfriends had in mind.

She shook off the silly thoughts and tried to focus on the television, but her gaze kept slipping back to the man, who was still looking at her little brother.

"You want to bring me some of that newspaper from your mom's crystal?"

"She's not my mom," Dillon said as he slid off the couch and retrieved the crumpled papers that Abby had tossed aside. He sidled over to the man, holding them out at arm's length.

She almost missed the speculative glance the man gave her before he took the paper from Dillon. He wadded it up and stuck it in the fireplace, between a couple of angled logs. "Got a match, bud?"

"Here." Abby quickly pulled a lighter out of her purse and carried it over.

"You smoke?" His tone was smooth, yet she still felt the accusation.

"You sound remarkably like my grandfather used to."

A full beat passed before his lips quirked. "My sister keeps telling me I'm getting old before my time," he said. "Must be true if I strike you as *grand*fatherly." He took the lighter and set the small flame to the newspaper. When he was sure it took, he straightened and left the lighter on the wood mantel.

"Abby's my sister," Dillon said so suddenly that she shot him a surprised look.

The man didn't look surprised. And he wasn't the least bit grandfatherly, though Abby didn't figure it would be appropriate to tell him so. He simply nodded at this additional information, not knowing how unusual it was for Dillon to offer anything where a stranger was concerned. He set the fireplace screen back in place. "What grade are you in?"

But her brother's bravery only went so far. He ducked his chin into his puffy down collar. "Second," he whispered and hurried back to the couch. He sat down on the edge of a cushion again and tucked his bare fingers under his legs.

Abby knew the best thing for Dillon was to keep things as normal as possible. So she ignored the way he was carefully looking away from them and focused on the tall man as he straightened. She was wearing flat-heeled snow boots, and he had at least a foot on her five-one. Probably a good eighty pounds, too, judging by the breadth of his shoulders. "Do you have kids?" Maybe a second-grader who'd become friends with Dillon.

"Nope." Which didn't really tell her whether there was a *wife* or not. "How much more do you need to unload?"

She followed him onto the porch. "A few boxes and our suitcases."

He grabbed the shovel as he went down the steps and

shoved it into the snow, pushing it ahead of him like a plow as he made his way to the car.

"You don't have to do that," Abby said quickly, following in his wake.

"Somebody needs to."

Her defenses prickled. "I appreciate the gesture, but I'm perfectly capable of shoveling my own driveway."

His dark gaze roved over her. "But you didn't. And I'm guessing if you'd *had* a shovel in that little car of yours, you'd have already used it so you could get the car into the driveway."

Since that was true, she didn't really have a response. "My grandfather had a snowblower," she said. "I didn't really have a good way to move it here, so I sold it." Along with most everything else that her grandparents had owned. Except the crystal. Ever since Abby had been a little girl, her grandmother had said that Abby would have it one day.

And now she did.

The reality of it all settled like a sad knot in her stomach.

She'd followed her grandfather's wishes. But that didn't mean it had been easy.

They'd lost him when he'd died of a heart attack two years earlier. But they'd been losing her grandmother by degrees for years before that. And in the past year, Minerva Marcum's Alzheimer's had become so advanced that she didn't even recognize Abby anymore.

Even though Abby was now a qualified RN, she'd had no choice but to do what her grandfather had made her promise to do when the time came—place her grandmother into full-time residential care.

"So you'll get another blower," the man was saying. "Or a shovel. But for now—" he waggled the long handle "—this is it." He set off again, pushing another long swath of snow clear from the driveway.

She trailed after him. "Mr., uh—"

"Sloan."

At last. A name. "Mr. Sloan, if you don't mind lending me the shovel, I can do that myself. I'm sure you've got better things to—"

"—just Sloan. And, no, I don't have better things to do. So go back inside, check the fire and unpack that crystal of yours. Soon as you can pull your car up in the driveway, I'll leave you to it."

She flopped her hands. "I can't stop you?"

"Evidently not." He reached the end of the driveway, pitched the snow to the side with enviable ease and turned to make another pass in the opposite direction. At the rate he was going, the driveway would be clear of the snow that reached halfway up her calves in a matter of minutes.

She ought to be grateful. Instead, she just felt inadequate. And she *hated* feeling inadequate.

Short of trying to wrestle the shovel out of his hands—which was a shockingly intriguing idea—she could either stand there watching or do something productive.

Like checking the fire and unpacking.

She went back inside. The fire had already started warming the room. Dillon had shed his coat and was sitting on the beige carpet, setting his video games neatly inside the cabinet. "When're we gonna visit Grandma?"

Abby stepped around his plastic crate and went to the fireplace. "I thought we'd go next weekend." She moved the fire screen aside and took a piece of wood from the stack. She jabbed the end of it against the burning logs, sending up a blur of sparks before tossing it onto the top. Then she replaced the screen and straightened. "We can't go every day like we used to."

"I know." He pushed out his lower lip, studying the cover of his video game. "Would she 'member us if Grandpa hadn't died?"

Abby sat down on the floor next to him, pulled off her coat and put her arm around him. "No, honey. Losing Grandpa has nothing to do with it. But we remember her." She ignored the tightening in her throat. "And we'll visit her every chance we can, just like I've told you. Okay?"

She felt his nod against her cheek.

"Okay." She pressed her lips to his forehead before pushing to her feet. "Why don't we leave the rest of our unpacking until later and get the television hooked up. I'm finally going to beat you at 'White Hats.'"

He snorted softly. "Yeah, right."

Which just eased the tightness in her throat and made her smile instead. She turned away from him only to stop short at the sight of Sloan standing inside the door. She hadn't even heard him open it.

"Driveway's clear."

She pulled at the hem of her long sweater. "Thank you. I'll have to figure out a way to return the favor."

His dark gaze seemed to sharpen. And maybe it was her imagination that his eyes flicked from her head to her toes, but then that would mean it was also her imagination that her stomach was swooping around. And she'd never been particularly prone to flights of imagination.

"That might be interesting." Then he smiled faintly and went out the door again, silently closing it after him.

Abby blinked. Let out a long breath.

If Mr. Just-Sloan *did* have a wife, he had no business making new neighbors feel breathless like that.

"Come on, Abby," Dillon said behind her. "I wanna play 'White Hats.'"

"I know. I know."

And if he doesn't have a wife?

She ignored the voice inside her head and pulled the television out of the box.

Whether the man was married or not didn't matter.

All she wanted to do was start her new job at the elementary school and raise Dillon with as much love as her grandparents had raised her.

Nothing more. Nothing less.

So she carried the new television over to the cabinet and began hooking it up. In minutes, the distinctive music from Dillon's video game was blasting through the speakers. He handed her a controller and she sat cross-legged on the carpet next to him as she set about trying not to be bested yet again by a seven-year-old.

She was no more successful at that than she was at not thinking about the man next door.

Chapter Two

"Sloan, it's New Year's Eve. You shouldn't be spending it alone," his sister, the voice of reason, said through the phone at his ear.

"I'm not interested in crashing your evening with Axel." Even though Tara had been married to the man for a few years now—had two kids with him, even—it was still hard for Sloan to say his brother-in-law's name without feeling a healthy dose of dislike. Axel Clay was part of the darkest time of Sloan's life. His sister being happily married to him made the situation tolerable. Barely. If not for that, Sloan could have gone the rest of his life hating the man. No more than he hated himself, though.

"You wouldn't be crashing anything, Bean." Tara laughed. "Most of the family's going to be here. It's not like Axel and I will have a chance to be romantic while there's a half-dozen kids chasing each other around."

Bean. The nickname she'd called him when they were

kids. Considering everything that Sloan had put her through—the disruption he'd caused in her life by the choices he'd made in his—it was a wonder that she could even recall the days when he'd been her Bean and she'd been his Goober.

They were twins. And they'd grown up in a family that never stayed in one place for more than a few months at a time. As an adult, all Tara had ever wanted was a stable place to call her own. While Sloan had kept right on with the rootless lifestyle.

Which was why he was living here in Weaver at all. Trying to make up for the acts of his past. Trying to make things right with the only female left in his life that he loved.

"Fine," he said. "I also don't want to crash your evening with the entire Clay clan." He looked out the front window of his house again. Abby had finally moved her car into the driveway. "Maybe I have plans of my own."

He could almost hear Tara's ears perk. "What plans would those be? Sitting in the dark, staring morosely into a beer while you dwell on the past?"

Almost guiltily, he set aside the frosted beer mug he was holding. "You don't know everything, Goob."

She sighed noisily. "Oh, all right. But you're not getting off the hook tomorrow. Dinner at the big house. You've already agreed, and if you try to back out, I'll call Max and sic him on you."

"My boss may be your cousin-in-law, but that doesn't mean he's gonna let you tell him what to do." In Sloan's estimation, nobody told Max Scalise what to do, not even the voters who put him in office term after term.

"We'll see," Tara countered. "Squire's expecting everyone for New Year's dinner, and nobody wants to cross *him*. Not even the mighty sheriff."

Squire Clay was Tara's grandfather-in-law and the patriarch of the large Clay family. He was older than dirt. Cantankerous as hell. And one of a few people in Weaver that Sloan could say he genuinely liked.

"I said I'd be there tomorrow and I will." A flash of red caught his eye, and he watched Abby bounce down the porch steps. But instead of heading toward her car, she started crossing the snow separating their houses.

"But tonight is mine," he finished. Up close, Abby had looked even younger than he'd expected, but she'd also had the prettiest gray eyes he'd ever seen.

"Okay. Happy New Year, Sloan," his sister said. "I'm glad you're here."

He pinched the bridge of his nose. He wished he could say the same, but he didn't know what he felt. If anything. "Happy New Year, kiddo."

Then he hung up and watched Abby cross in front of the window where he was standing. A second later, she knocked on his front door.

He left his beer on the table and answered the door.

"Hi." Those gray eyes of hers looked up at him, carrying the same cheerfulness that infused the smile on her soft, pink lips. "Sorry to bother you."

"You're not." He leaned his shoulder against the doorjamb. He ought to feel like a letch, admiring her the way he was. But he didn't. He felt…interested.

The first time he'd felt interested in longer than he cared to remember.

"What d'you need?"

"Wood, actually."

The devil on his shoulder laughed at that one. No problem there. The angel on his other shoulder had him straightening away from the doorjamb. "It's back behind the house." He pushed the door open wide. "Come on in."

The tip of her tongue peeked out to flick over her upper lip. "Thanks." She stepped past him into the house, and he saw the way her gaze took in the sparsely furnished living room. "Hope I'm not interrupting anything."

"Nope." He led the way through the room to the kitchen at the back of the house and outside again. He gestured at the woodpile stacked next to the back steps, protected from the weather by the overhang of the roof. "Help yourself."

She went down the steps, her shiny hair swaying around her shoulders. He shoved his fingers into the pockets of his jeans and tried not to think how silky her hair would feel.

"Thanks again." She stacked several pieces of wood in her arms. "I'll restock as soon as I can."

"No need." Thanks to his connection to the Clay family and their gigantic cattle ranch, the Double-C, he had a ready supply of firewood, whether he wanted it or not. "House warming up okay over there?"

She nodded. Her hair bounced. Her eyes smiled.

She'd have the boys at the elementary and junior high schools sticking their fingers down their throats just to have a chance to visit her in the nurse's office.

The devil on his shoulder laughed at him again. *Wouldn't you do the same?*

"Your brother live with you all the time?" Sloan was betting the "brother" story was just that. The boy looked just like her. He was probably her son. Which would mean she'd had him very, *very* young.

"Yes." She lifted the load in her arms and started backing away, making fresh tracks in the snow. "Thanks for this. Hope you and your wife enjoy the rest of your evening."

Interesting. "Who said there's a wife?"

Her gaze skipped away. "Just assuming." She smiled again. Kept backing away. Right until she bumped into the side of her house. She laughed and began sidestepping instead.

"Assuming wrong."

She hesitated. Just for a moment, before continuing right along. But it had been long enough for him to notice.

Definitely interesting.

"Ah. Well." She clutched the logs to her chest. "Hope you enjoy the rest of *your* evening, then." Her smile never faltered.

He wondered if it ever did. She had a face made for smiles.

"You, too."

She reached the end of the fence and finally turned away, crossing into her front yard.

Her hair swayed and bounced.

Sloan shook his head and went back inside. Whether or not the boy was her brother or her son, a young woman like Abby Marcum didn't need something temporary in her life.

And temporary was all he had to offer.

The car was unloaded. Most of the boxes unpacked.

Abby sat on the wooden barstool at her breakfast bar and looked at Dillon. He was sprawled on the couch, a fleecy blanket pulled up to his chin, sound asleep. He'd had his triumph at 'White Hats.' Had his popcorn. Had the casserole she'd managed to throw together.

It was nearly midnight. She could have gone to bed herself.

She sighed and poked through the box of chocolates, selected one and followed it up with a chaser of milk. She doubted her girlfriends would approve. They'd also sent her away with a bottle of champagne. It was sitting, unopened, in the refrigerator.

No champagne and no horizontal entertainment for her,

both of which they'd insisted it was high time she finally experience.

She held up her grandmother's delicate crystal flute and stared at the milk. "Happy New Year," she murmured just as the lights flickered twice then went out completely.

With the television silent, all she could hear was the ticking of the clock that she'd hung on the kitchen wall and the faint hiss from the log burning in the fireplace.

By firelight, she leisurely finished her milk and waited for the electricity to come back on. When it didn't, she retrieved the lighter from the mantel where Sloan had left it and lit several candles.

Then she headed back to the barstool and the chocolates.

There was a loud knock on her door as she picked up the gold box. And at that hour it was certainly unexpected. But it wasn't alarm that had her hurrying to the door; it was the fact that she didn't want Dillon waking up. He was sleeping so soundly, and she didn't want to ruin it. It was a rare night that passed without him waking out of a bad dream.

She cracked open the door and looked out. Sloan stood there, a sturdy flashlight in his hand, and she opened the door wider. The air outside felt bracingly cold in comparison to the warmth slipping through her at the sight of him.

"Everything okay here?"

"Fine." She poked her head out the door, looking up and down the darkened street. "Why?"

"Just making sure."

"It's only a power outage." She smiled. "Did you think I'd be over here shaking in my boots?"

The beam of his flashlight shifted, moving across her bare feet. "You're not wearing boots."

She curled her toes against the carpet. "You caught me." She realized she was still holding the gold box and extended it. "Care for one?"

"I don't know." His deep voice was amused. "There was a time when my mother told me not to take candy from strangers."

Abby grinned. "Wise woman. But it's your loss. These aren't just ordinary chocolates." She held the box up a little higher. In the glow from the flashlight, he couldn't fail to notice the distinctive box. "You sure? I promised the friends who gave them to me that I'd share them with someone other than Dillon."

"I see. Can't have you breaking a promise, then." He raised his flashlight and took one.

"No point in standing out in the cold. Come on in. I'll get you something to drink." And then she held her breath, because she was pretty sure that he wouldn't accept her invitation.

But he stepped past her.

Her stomach swooped.

She noticed that Dillon still hadn't moved as she quietly closed the door before crossing to the bar again. "Have a seat." She waved at the second barstool and set the chocolates on the counter.

He shut off his flashlight and shrugged out of his jacket. "Looks like you're putting your grandmother's crystal to good use."

"Trying." She got a second flute from the cupboard then pulled open the refrigerator and snatched the champagne. She set the glass and the bottle in front of him. "You'll need to open it, I'm afraid." She didn't even know how.

He tilted his head slightly as he picked up the crystal flute she'd been using. Candlelight danced over it. "Definitely doesn't look like you're drinking champagne."

She felt silly. Grown women didn't drink milk out of champagne glasses. "I'm not."

He lifted her glass to his nose. The old crystal looked shockingly delicate in his long fingers. "You mind?" But he didn't wait to see if she did; he simply took a sip. Right from her glass.

Her mouth suddenly felt very dry, and she sat down weakly on her own barstool. The width of the counter separated them, but she still felt dwarfed by him. It wasn't just that he was tall. His shoulders were massive. And up close like this, she was pretty sure she could make out a tattoo of some sort on his neck, not quite hidden by the neckline of his long-sleeved T-shirt.

"Milk always goes well with chocolate," he murmured. He set her glass down on the counter and slid it toward her. "That's what I'll have if you've got enough to share."

She nodded, afraid that if she tried to speak, her voice would just come out as one long squeak. She went back to the fridge, blindly snatched the milk carton and filled his glass.

"Anything else your friends say you're supposed to do besides share the chocolate?" He kept his voice low, and even though she knew it was because of Dillon, it still felt unbearably intimate.

She picked up her own glass. She couldn't lie to save her soul, and there was no way she'd share what they'd told her about finally having sex, so she just grazed the side of her glass against his. "Cheers," she whispered instead.

"Not exactly an answer, Abby."

"I guess it isn't. What'd you say your name was?"

His teeth flashed in the dim light. "Sloan McCray," he finally offered.

And just like that, she realized why he'd seemed familiar. Because she'd seen his face before in the newspapers. On the television news. On the internet.

He looked different from the clean-cut man in the snapshots she remembered, but she was certain he was the undercover ATF agent who'd brought down the horrendous Deuce's Cross gang a few years ago. She remembered watching the news stories on the television in her grandfather's hospital room. Sloan had succeeded at something no one before him had been able to do. He was a hero.

And he was sitting right here, watching her with narrowed eyes, as if he were waiting for some reaction.

She got the sense that if she gave one, he'd bolt.

So she didn't.

"So, Sloan McCray," she said softly. "Why aren't you out celebrating New Year's Eve somewhere?"

"I am out celebrating." He tilted the glass and drank down half of the milk.

She couldn't help grinning, even though she was afraid it made her look like a cartoon character.

He set the glass down again and pulled the gold box closer so he could study the contents. He'd folded one arm on the counter and was leaning toward her. "Anything besides the job bringing you and Dillon to Weaver?"

"No." She realized she'd mirrored his position when he looked up from the box and their heads were only inches apart. Her heart raced around fiendishly inside her chest. "We lived in Braden, but working at the school here was too good an opportunity to pass up. I'll have essentially the same hours as Dillon." Her grandfather had planned well, but that didn't mean Abby could afford to spend money on after-school care if she didn't need to.

"And you want to stay close to Braden," Sloan concluded. "For your grandmother."

"You did overhear that."

He nodded once. Took another sip of milk, watching her over the rim of the flute.

"What about you? What brings you to Weaver?"

"Maybe I come from here."

If she recalled correctly, the news stories had said he'd hailed from Chicago. "*Do* you?"

He didn't answer immediately. He selected a chocolate. Studied it. "My sister lives here," he finally said. Then he turned his back to her and stood.

Disappointment flooded her, but all he did was walk across to the fireplace and quietly place another piece of wood on the dying embers. Then he returned to his bar-stool. He held up his nearly empty glass. "Unless you've got more, we might need to open that champagne after all."

"I have more," she said quickly and retrieved the milk carton. She filled his glass, emptying the carton.

"You're not going to have any left for Dillon in the morning."

She curled her toes around the wooden ring near the base of her barstool. "He likes brown sugar and raisins on his oatmeal anyway."

His lips twitched. "That's the way my mother used to fix oatmeal for us. What else did you leave behind in Braden?"

Her mouth went dry all over again at the way he was looking at her, his eyes so dark and hooded. "I tried to bring everything that mattered."

"Grandma's crystal." He held up his glass.

"And Grandpa's shotgun." She smiled. "Safely stowed away in a cabinet, well out of Dillon's reach. Plus his video games. Dillon's that is, not my grandfather's." She was babbling but couldn't help herself. "Photographs. Clothes."

"You're not answering my real question. You have a boyfriend waiting for you in Braden? Some nice kid as fresh-faced and wet behind the ears as you?"

She didn't know whether to be charmed or insulted. "I'm neither a kid nor wet behind the ears."

He gave that slight half smile again. "How old are you?"

She moistened her lips. "Twenty-three."

He made a face. "I've got ten years on you."

She managed to hide her surprise. He was ungodly handsome, but his face held far more wear than any man in his early thirties should. She guessed that was the price for the kind of work he'd done. "In any case, no, there is no one waiting for me to come home to Braden." She plucked a chocolate from the box and shoved it into her mouth with no regard for its fineness. "No boyfriend. No husband. No nothing," she said around its melting sweetness. "Been too busy raising Dillon for the past two years. Even if there had been time, I'm still a package deal."

His eyebrows rose. "Where are your parents?"

She lifted her shoulders. "Who knows? He's my half brother. We share the same mother, but she was no more interested in raising him than she was me. Which is why—"

"The grandparents," he concluded.

She nodded. "What about your parents?"

The devil laughed mockingly in Sloan's ear. That was what he got for showing some curiosity about Abby. She naturally showed some curiosity in return. "They died when my sister and I were twenty," he said abruptly. Tara had turned into a homebody after their childhood, and he had been the opposite. But he knew they shared the same distaste for talking about that childhood.

"That must have been hard."

Not any harder than growing up without parents at all, which seemed to be the case for her. He folded his arms on the counter again, leaning closer. Close enough to smell the clean fragrance of her shining brown hair. "You start work when the holiday break is over?"

"In two days. At least it'll be a short week."

"Nervous?"

She shook her head. Made a face. "Guess it shows, huh?"

"You'll be fine."

She toyed with her glass for a moment. "What do you do?"

"Deputy sheriff. For the next few months, anyway." He didn't know what the hell had him offering that last bit. Maybe a thin attempt to lay some groundwork. Some *temporary* groundwork.

"What happens after that?"

He hesitated and wasn't sure what he would have said if the electricity hadn't kicked on just then. Light from the overhead fixture flooded the kitchen, and the television came to life.

"Look," she whispered, leaning to the side to peer around him. "The ball in New York is nearly down."

He glanced over his shoulder. Sure enough, the TV showed the famed crystal ball inching its way down while a mass of people around it cheered and screamed.

"Three." He turned back to watch Abby, whose gray gaze was focused on the countdown.

"Two," she whispered on a smile.

"One," he finished.

Her pretty eyes lifted to his. "Happy New Year, Sloan."

Maybe it was the devil. Maybe it was the angel.

Maybe it was just him.

"It is now," he murmured. And he leaned the last few inches across the counter and slowly pressed his mouth against hers.

Chapter Three

Shocked, Abby inhaled sharply.

He tasted like dark chocolate. Cold milk.

And things that she'd never experienced and suddenly wanted to, so very badly.

But just when she was adjusting to the notion that Sloan McCray's lips were brushing across *hers,* he was lifting his head. "Next time you talk to your friends, you can tell them that you lived up to your promise."

He meant sharing the chocolate, of course. But she couldn't do a single thing except sit there and mutely nod.

The lines arrowing out from the corners of his dark eyes crinkled a little. "You pour a helluva cocktail," he murmured before turning away and walking silently to the door.

A moment later, he was gone.

And Abby was *still* sitting there as mute as a stump of wood.

"Izzit New Year's?" Dillon's sleepy voice startled her so much she jumped off her stool as if she'd been stung. She rounded the counter and went over to the couch where he was knuckling his eyes.

"It is. And time for *you* to go to bed, Mr. Marcum."

He giggled a little, the way he always did when she called him that. "I stayed awake the whole time, didn't I," he boasted as he slid off the couch, dragging his blanket after him.

"Sure thing, honey."

He padded barefoot into the first bedroom. "I think Mr. Sloan is a White Hat," he said.

She folded back the comforter for Dillon to climb into bed. It was noticeably cooler in his room than in the living room, but the comforter would keep him warm enough. "Why's that?" The video game was the classic story of good against evil. White Hats against Black Hats. Of course in this instance, it was geared for children, so the hats were worn by animated dinosaurs. Dillon loved all things dinosaur.

Her little brother shrugged as he climbed onto his twin-size bed. "'Cause."

"Sounds like a good reason to me." She brushed his dark hair off his forehead and kissed him. "Go to sleep. Oatmeal with raisins in the morning."

He threw his arms tightly around her neck. "You're not gonna leave, too, are you, Abby?"

Her heart squeezed. He didn't mean leave his bedroom. He meant *leave*.

"I'm not ever going to leave," she promised. She smacked a kiss on both of his cheeks and settled him against his pillow. "Ever," she added.

He let out a long breath as if her answer had actually

been in doubt then grabbed his fleece blanket up against his cheek and turned onto his side.

Abby left his room, pulling the door halfway closed so that he'd still be able to see the light from the bathroom next door.

Then she returned to the living room, blew out all the candles and cleaned up, washing and drying the crystal glasses carefully before putting them back in the cupboard.

Seeing that the fire was burning low and steadily, safely contained by the screen, she shut off the lights in preparation of going to bed herself.

Instead of going to her own room, though, she found herself at the front window, peering into the darkness.

She touched her fingertips to her lips.

Felt her stomach swoop around.

It was a first for her.

Oh, not the kiss. She'd been kissed before. Just never at midnight. Never on New Year's Eve.

But she needed to remember that to Sloan McCray, the kiss was probably nothing more than a simple gesture.

She looked at the house next door. Wondered where his bedroom was. Wondered if he was thinking about her, too.

But then she shook her head. He'd called her "wet behind the ears." And the way she was standing there, gazing at his house in the darkness, would only prove that she was. So she turned on her heels and went into her bedroom across the hall from Dillon's.

Her bed wasn't the narrow twin that Dillon's was, but it was just as innocent. She peeled off her leggings and her sweater and pulled open her drawer. Her pj's were about as seductive as Dillon's, too. Soft cotton pants with pink-and-green polka dots and a matching T-shirt with a grinning skunk on the front of it.

She made a face as she changed and threw herself down on the middle of her full-size bed.

Her room was even chillier than Dillon's, but she felt hot. Flushed. It didn't take a genius to figure out why.

Even before learning that the man next door was a true-life American hero, he'd made her stomach swoop.

She stared into the darkness and pressed her fingertips to her lips again.

Then she groaned and flipped onto her side, hugging the pillow to her cheek.

The mattress springs squeaked slightly when Sloan flipped restlessly onto his back for the tenth time.

Dawn was finally relieving the darkness seeping around the blinds, and instead of lying there, tossing and turning pointlessly for another few hours, he pushed off the bed and went to the window. He tilted the blinds just enough so that he could look down on the house next door.

Did the window on the side of the house belong to her bedroom or Dillon's?

He muttered a low oath. Kissing her had been stupid.

Sweet as all get-out.

But still stupid.

Abby Marcum was a nice girl. And, sweet lips or not, she was not what he needed in his life.

He didn't know what he needed. But he knew it was not a girl like her. A girl with responsibilities. With ties. The kind of girl who'd expect ties.

As well she should.

If there was one thing Sloan was not good at, it was ties. He was trying where Tara was concerned, but even with his own sister he wasn't winning any awards.

He turned away from the window, dragged on his running gear and went outside. The air was frozen, sending his breath into clouds around his head as he stretched. He usually ran in the middle of the night. Maybe that was crazy, but it was better than tossing and turning while sleeplessness drove him nuts.

Last night, though, he'd been busy looking into Abby's open, innocent face.

He shut down those thoughts and set off down the street in the opposite direction from the one he usually went, just so he wouldn't pass by her house.

Instead, he ended up passing the school where Dillon would be going in a few days, and where she'd be handing out bandages and ice packs, and he thought about her anyway.

He picked up his pace and headed around to Main Street. Light was already streaming from the windows of Ruby's Café. New Year's Day or not, Tabby Taggart was obviously already at work in the kitchen, probably making the fresh sweet rolls that people came for from miles away. He knew that she'd already have hot coffee brewing and if he knocked on the window, she'd let him in.

He kept running and passed the darkened windows of his sister's shop, Classic Charms. Even though she'd taken on a partner now, he still thought of the shop as Tara's. He finally slowed as he reached the sheriff's office and went inside to the warmth and the smell of coffee there.

The dispatcher, Pam Rasmussen, gave him a look over the reading glasses perched on her nose. "Surprise, surprise. Some of us come into the office because we're scheduled on duty. Others, namely you, come in because you have nothing better to do."

"Happy New Year to you, too. And I'm not here to work. I was just out for a run." He reached across her desk and flipped the book she was reading so he could see the cover. "Suppose that's another one of those romances you like."

"What if it is? *Romance* isn't a dirty word. If you realized that, maybe you wouldn't go around so grumpy all the time. I know plenty of women who'd—"

"*No,*" he cut her off bluntly. The last thing he needed was a setup by her. Or by his sister. Or by anyone.

The taste of dark, creamy chocolate on Abby's lips taunted him, and he ruthlessly closed his mind to it. "Quiet night?"

"Except for a call out at the Pierce place." She grimaced. "Neighbors called in the disturbance."

Sloan filled his mug and glanced around the office. All of the desks were empty. "Who took the call?"

"Ruiz. Just before he got off shift. Report's still on his desk if you want to read it."

Dave Ruiz was one of the other deputies at the Weaver office. There were more than twenty of them in all, covering the county.

"Dawson's out on an accident toward Braden, and Jerry's checking an alarm that went off at the medical offices next to Shop-World," Pam added, without looking up from her book.

Sloan picked up the report on the Pierce disturbance, read through it and tossed it back down again. "Lorraine Pierce needs to leave that bastard," he said.

"Yup." Pam turned a page in her book. "But she won't. Not until he puts her in the hospital. Or worse."

Sloan sighed. He figured Pam was probably right. And there wasn't a damn thing they could do because Lorraine refused to admit that her husband, Bobby, had hurt or threatened her in any way. Every time they'd locked him up, she'd taken him home again. "She ought to put some thought into that kid of hers, then," he muttered. Calvin Pierce was about Dillon's age.

Which only had him thinking about Abby yet again.

He gulped down the coffee, scorching the lining of his

mouth in the process. But not even that managed to eradicate the image of Abby's soft eyes staring up at him over a crystal glass full of milk.

"When're you gonna tell Max you'll stay on for good?"

He looked over at Pam. She was still reading her book.

The sheriff had asked him to stay on permanently, but Sloan wasn't ready to agree. "Guess that's between me and Max."

She tilted her head, eyeing him over the top of her reading glasses. She just smiled slightly. Pam was not only the department's dispatcher, she was also one of the biggest gossips in town, and he didn't want to provide the woman with any more fodder than necessary.

He took his coffee, went into the locker room and grabbed a shower. Then he dressed in jeans and an old ATF sweatshirt, signed out his usual cruiser and drove back home through the thin morning light.

Abby's house was still dark when he turned into his driveway a few minutes later. No signs that they were up and about or that the oatmeal with raisins was in progress.

He went inside and started a pot of coffee and tried to pretend that the house next to him was still sitting empty and cold and unoccupied.

He was no more successful at that than he was trying to decide what to do with his life.

"Abby, come *on*." Dillon was dancing around on his snow-booted feet, impatiently waiting for her to finish putting away the breakfast dishes. "You promised we'd make a snowman. With a carrot nose and everything."

Her brother was a lot more enthusiastic about trudging around in the snow for a few hours than she was. But she'd promised, so she rounded the breakfast counter and tugged his stocking cap down over his eyes, making him giggle. "You can get started while I put on my coat."

He pushed his hat back and raced out the front door, so anxious that he didn't even pull it shut behind him. She followed and stuck her head out. "Stay in our yard," she started to warn needlessly. Dillon was already crouching down next to the porch, balling up a handful of snow in his mittens to begin the snowman.

Her gaze shifted to the house next door.

It was completely still, not even showing a spiral of smoke from the chimney like most of the other houses on the block. She would have assumed he was gone, if not for the SUV emblazoned with Sheriff on the side parked in his driveway.

"Hurry *up,* Abby!"

Dragging her eyes away from the house next door, she noticed that Dillon's snowball had already grown to the size of a pumpkin. She retrieved her own coat and boots and, when she was bundled up almost as much as her brother, went outside.

The pumpkin had nearly doubled in diameter by the time she joined Dillon in the middle of the yard. "How big are you planning to make that?"

He threw his arms wide. "This big."

She couldn't help laughing. "You want a *fat* snowman, then. All right." She bent over and put her gloved hands against the big ball. "Let's roll, bud."

Even between the two of them, by the time they managed to push the growing ball across the yard twice more, they could barely manage to budge it. "This is big enough," she told him breathlessly as she straightened. Her breath clouded around her head, but warm from their exertions, she pulled off her knit cap and shoved it into her pocket.

"No, it's not," Dillon argued. He threw his arms wide again. "*This* big."

"Dillon—"

"Kid's right," a deep voice said behind them. "It's no-where near big enough."

She whirled to see Sloan standing on his front porch watching them. Pleasure exploded in her veins.

He'd kissed her.

On New Year's Eve at midnight, he'd kissed her.

Maybe it meant nothing to him, but it sure had meant something to her.

"Happy New Year," she said brightly. Despite the frigid temperature, he was wearing only a long-sleeved black sweatshirt with his jeans. "Aren't you cold?"

There was at least fifty feet separating their houses, but she could still see his wry smile from where she stood. "Watching all that work you're doing's keeping me warm enough."

Not entirely sure what to make of that, she felt herself flush. Dillon was bouncing around his snowman base, and she focused on that. "We can't make this any bigger," she told them both. "It's already too heavy to move."

"Mr. Sloan'll help," Dillon said. He peered up at Sloan. "Wontcha?"

"Dillon," Abby cautioned quickly. She was still surprised at Dillon's unusual openness where their new neighbor was concerned. "Mr. *McCray* might have other things to do right now. It's New Year's Day, remember? It's a holiday. People usually spend holidays with their families or friends."

Dillon's lower lip pushed out. "We're not with our family. And maybe he's a friend."

She didn't dare glance at Sloan. "We just met Mr. Mc-

Cray yesterday." Kiss or not, it was too early to tell just what Sloan McCray was to them, besides their neighbor.

"Every time you say Mr. McCray, I want to look around my shoulder for my old man."

"I suppose it really should be Deputy McCray, anyway."

"You're a *deputy?*" Dillon's voice went up a notch. "Do you got a gun and a badge?"

"I do, though I don't much care for the gun part." Sloan had come down his steps. He was carrying a silver thermal cup in one bare hand, and his eyes narrowed slightly as he took a drink of its contents while he crossed the yard. "And I think just calling me Sloan will do."

Considering the heat rising inside her, Abby wanted to unwind the scarf from around her neck and ditch it, too, but she resisted the urge. Dillon would think he could do the same, and he was plagued with winter colds. "You need a coat," she told Sloan. She also didn't want Dillon thinking he could emulate the tall man from next door, either. "At least some gloves."

"I didn't get to come out without *my* coat," Dillon said. With his stocking cap, his puffy down coat, his scarf and his mittens, his skinny little body was nearly round.

"And we've got to do as Nurse Marcum says," Sloan drawled. He pulled a pair of black gloves from his back pocket. "Think these'll do?"

She knew she was blushing. "Not unless they're on your hands."

His amusement turned to an outright smile, confirming what she already knew. Spectacular. Definitely spectacular.

And she felt entirely caught in the spell of his brown eyes.

"Hold this." He handed her the thermal mug and pulled

on his gloves, his gaze finally sliding away to focus on Dillon.

"Your sister needs to see what the men can do," Sloan was saying to Dillon, who beamed in response. He crouched next to the boulder-sized snowball. Dillon did the same, and they began rolling the ball, not stopping until it was even more enormous.

Abby dragged her gaze from the view of Sloan's backside before he straightened. "Good thing you finally stopped," she offered. "Or there wouldn't be enough snow left on the ground to make the other two parts of Mr. Frosty, here." She held out the mug, but Sloan waved it off.

"Dillon, you start on the head," he suggested. "Your sister and I will work on the middle."

"He's gotta have a *fat* belly," Dillon warned.

"I think we can manage," Sloan assured him. His gaze met Abby's. "Or did you just want to sit on the porch looking pretty while the men slave away?"

"I was working hard enough on the base before you appeared." She set the mug on one of the porch steps.

Did he really think she was pretty?

Embarrassed by her own thoughts, she scooped up a handful of snow, packing it down tightly to start the midsection. Sloan added to it until it was so large she needed both hands to hold it. Then they rolled it around on the ground until it was almost as big as the base and they had to wrestle it into place. Once they had it where they wanted it, Sloan lifted Dillon so he could put the head he'd formed on top.

When they were done, Abby stood back and laughed. Dillon's snowman head was woefully small in proportion to the rest of the monster.

"I'm gonna get the carrot!" Dillon raced into the house.

Sloan moved next to Abby, and she went still when he unwound the scarf from her neck. "What are you doing?"

"Not trying to undress you in the middle of your front yard," he murmured dryly.

Her cheeks went hot. "I didn't—"

"Not that undressing you doesn't hold plenty of appeal."

Her lips snapped shut. She feared her face was as red as her coat.

He smiled slightly. "But a snowman needs a scarf, doesn't he?" He finally turned away and wrapped the scarf around the snowman's neck. The candy-cane-striped knit fluttered cheerfully against the enormously oversize midsection.

Dillon's boots clomped on the porch as he returned. He clutched a long carrot in his fist and reached up to jab it squarely in the center of the snowman's face. "What're we gonna use for eyes?"

"When I was a kid, we always used buttons. But we don't have any spares anymore." Abby thought about the old jelly jar her grandmother had once used to store spare buttons.

Even though she looked away quickly, Sloan still caught the sudden shimmer in Abby's eyes.

Fortunately, Dillon hadn't noticed because he was too enamored of his snowy creation. Sloan gestured at his house. "I have a bag of cookies on my kitchen counter," he told the boy. "Run over and grab a few. They'll work for eyes."

But the boy didn't race off the way Sloan figured he would. He sidled next to Abby. "Should I?" he heard him ask under his breath.

She brushed her fingers over the cap on his head. "Do you want me to go with you?"

The boy ducked his chin into his coat and gave Sloan a look from the corner of his eye. "He's really a *deputy?*"

Abby nodded. She smiled at Sloan, but it didn't hold a fraction of the brilliance that he knew it could. That it should.

"Look at the truck in his driveway," she told her brother. "It says Sheriff on the side and everything."

Dillon looked. After a moment, his chin came out of his coat. "I can go myself," he announced. Evidently, *deputy* and *sheriff* were the encouragement he needed.

"Bring a couple extra cookies," Sloan suggested. "I think we need to eat a few after all this hard work."

Dillon nodded and headed across the yard with the care of someone crossing a minefield.

"He's pretty serious for a little kid."

"You would be too if you'd had a mother like ours." Abby didn't look at him but fussed with the scarf around the snowman's neck. "I was lucky. She dumped me off on her parents when I was a baby. She chose to hold on to Dillon until he was four."

"And then she booked."

Abby nodded. "Don't know where. Don't care why." Her face was open. Honest.

"But you care about buttons."

"Dillon's too serious, and you're too observant."

"County pays me to be observant."

Her lips curved sadly. "This is the first New Year's that I haven't spent with my grandmother. Every year before she got sick, she'd make black-eyed peas for good luck and roast a turkey with all the fixings." She looked past him toward the door that Dillon had disappeared through. "She used to save her buttons in a jelly jar. When I was little, I'd string them into necklaces and bracelets." She shrugged. "Probably sounds silly."

"Sounds like good memories."

Her expression softened. And he had a strong urge just to fall into the soft, gray warmth of her eyes. "They are good memories. Thanks for reminding me of that."

He took a step toward her, not even sure what he was after, but Dillon returned with all of the speed that had been missing when he went into the house. He was holding up a handful of chocolate sandwich cookies. "We gotta put the eyes in! Otherwise, Deputy Frosty can't see anything."

Abby caught the corner of her lip between her teeth, and her eyes smiled into Sloan's. "He's been promoted to deputy already? What are we going to do for a badge?"

"I'll draw him one." Stretching, Dillon worked the cookies into the snow above the carrot nose. They were a little uneven but seemed to suit the small-headed, big-bellied guy.

"What about his mouth?" Abby asked.

"He don't need a mouth."

"Sure he does," Sloan argued. "What if a pretty snow-girl came by and wanted to kiss him?" He enjoyed watching the pink color bloom in Abby's cheeks.

Dillon, however, wrinkled his nose. "Kissing's gross."

Sloan hid a smile. "Depends on the snowgirl, kid."

"Now I see why you're not still hanging around the office on your day off."

Sloan looked over his shoulder to see Pam Rasmussen sitting in her SUV, the window rolled down. She was grinning like the cat who'd gotten the cream. "Looks like y'all are having fun."

He didn't want to imagine the speculation going on inside the dispatcher's busy mind as he started to provide the briefest of introductions.

But they turned out to be unnecessary when Abby crossed the lawn and shook Pam's hand through the opened window. "I think we actually know each other through an old friend of mine from high school," she told her. "Delia Templeton?"

Pam clapped her hands together. "Of course!" Her gaze went past Abby to Sloan. "Delia's my cousin," she told him. "Well, my husband Rob's cousin, anyway. And now here you are, playing in the snow with one of our very own deputy sheriffs. What a small, small world."

Sloan could practically see the wheels turning inside Pam's head. "What're you doing here, Pam?" She and Rob lived on the other side of town.

"Doing a favor for my mom. She's been keeping an eye on her uncle's house while he's been gone." She gestured toward the house on the other side of Abby's where old Gilcrest lived. "He's coming back tomorrow, and she wanted the heat turned up for him. Told her I'd take care of it when my shift ended. Never expected to find a little romance brewing right next door." She smiled slyly as her SUV began slowly rolling forward. "Better get that heat going."

Sloan managed not to groan. "Don't pay her any attention," he told Abby as Pam drove a little farther and stopped in front of her uncle's house. "She's always like that."

"I know." Her head bobbed quickly. "Delia has shared loads of stories about her family. Everyone is into everyone's business." She looked over at Dillon, who'd lost interest in what the adults were doing and was sitting on the porch steps holding two chocolate cookies in front of his face as though they were his eyes. She grinned at the sight and looked back at Sloan. "Do you have plans for dinner today? I'm not fixing anything fancy—nothing like a turkey or black-eyed peas, but—"

"I do have plans," he cut her off abruptly then felt like a heel. He was aware of the way Pam was watching them as she walked up to the old man's house. "I promised my sister. Family dinner."

"Abby, I wanna make a badge for the snowman."

Her gray gaze cut away from his face to look at her brother. "Sure thing, honey." She glanced at Sloan again as she started toward the house. "Thanks for your help with the snowman. Hope you have a good time with your sister."

Given a choice, he'd have been happy to stay right where he was, with or without Pam's unwanted attention. There wasn't a romance brewing for the simple reason that he didn't do romance. No point.

But the heat? That was definitely already on.

Chapter Four

"Here." A longneck bottle appeared over Sloan's shoulder, and he looked back to see his brother-in-law standing there.

He wanted nothing from Axel, but he could see Tara watching them from across the living room of the Double-C's main house, where they'd all congregated after the New Year's Day feast. He accepted the bottle and clinked the bottom of it once against Axel's and turned his attention back to the football game playing on the wall-mounted television.

His hope that the other man would move along was blown when Axel sat down on the couch, too.

"Tara's worried you're going to book when your stint with Max is up."

He already knew that. But he was damned if he knew what to do about it when he couldn't even figure out what *he* wanted to do. He thought a little longingly of Abby's dinner. He wouldn't be having this conversation if he'd canceled on his sister and stayed with Abby and Dillon. But if he'd canceled, he'd just have another thing to regret where Tara was concerned. "Whether I stay or not doesn't have anything to do with Tara."

Axel grimaced. "Right, 'cause it has to do with me."

Sloan picked at the bottle label with his thumb. "I don't want to talk about this."

"Neither do I. But I love my wife. And she loves you."

"I've told her she needs to stop worrying about me."

Axel laughed shortly. "Yeah. That's going to happen. She's finally got you back. She doesn't want to lose you again."

"Whatever I decide, she's not going to lose me." He kept his focus on the television, even though the first half of the football game had just ended. "Undercover work for me is in the past." He hadn't merely worked undercover. He'd been deep undercover. So deep, and for so long, that the line between reality and fiction had gotten way too blurred.

Some days—most days—it still felt that way.

The record books would show a successful conclusion to the operation. A deadly gang had been dismantled. Murdering thieves had been imprisoned.

But in the end, Sloan's ATF career had been toast and the woman he'd loved—whom Axel Clay had been brought in to protect—had been dead.

He knew he couldn't lay the blame for Maria's death at Axel's door even if he wanted to. Sloan was the one who'd set that into motion when he'd told her the truth about what he was really doing. He hadn't wanted to lose her. But he'd lost her anyway when she'd tried going back to her old life once he'd taken his years of evidence to his bosses. If she hadn't known the truth about Sloan, they'd have left her alone. She wouldn't have been a possible witness in their eyes; she'd have just been the cocktail waitress they'd never had reason to distrust.

All she'd wanted to do was keep her life intact, but she'd paid a fatal price for it. Then it all seemed to be repeating itself when Sloan's sister suddenly found herself in the same sort of danger. It was Axel who'd succeeded in keeping Tara safe. Sloan was grateful for that, but he still knew it was his fault that she'd needed protecting in the first place.

He gave his brother-in-law a steady look. "Whether I stay or go doesn't have anything to do with you, either," he said evenly. "Or Maria," he made himself add. For his sister's sake. "Tara's good at putting down roots. I'm not."

"You're good at it when there's something that matters enough to you." Axel's tone was just as deliberate. "You spent a lot of years riding with Johnny Diablo and the Deuces." He scooped up his two-year-old son, Aidan, who was chasing full tilt after one of his older cousins. "Seems to me the question is what does matter that much to you?"

Sloan caught his nephew's wildly swinging foot before it connected with his face and tickled the bottom of it, making Aidan squeal. The little whirlwind managed to climb from his dad's lap to Sloan's back, where he clung like a monkey. "Ride! Ride!"

Glad for an excuse, Sloan rose from the couch. "Duty calls." He turned on his heel to give Axel's son his requested ride.

They went as far as the basement, which was as crowded as the upstairs living room. The main house was big, but so was the extensive Clay family. They had every age covered from babies to octogenarians.

"Gampa, Gampa, Gampa," Aidan yelled when he spotted Squire sitting amid a trio of young teenagers.

The old man handed his video-game controller to the

only girl in the trio. "Infernal game," he groused. But considering the way his face was creased with a grin, there wasn't a lot of bite to it.

Tristan Clay, who was the youngest and wealthiest of Squire's sons—and as far as Sloan was concerned, the wiliest—roused himself from his napping sprawl nearby. "That infernal game's putting a new wing on the hospital," he pointed out without heat.

Squire harrumphed. "Folks have always been willin' to throw good money away."

Tristan just smiled faintly, letting the jab pass.

It wasn't often that Sloan saw Tristan looking so relaxed. He ran his insanely successful video-gaming company, Cee-Vid, but he was also the number two man behind Hollins-Winword, an international firm that dealt in private security and covert intelligence. And it was in that role that Sloan had first dealt with the man and his nephew, Axel. Before he'd gone undercover with the Deuces, he'd asked Hollins-Winword to watch over Tara. She still hadn't quite forgiven him for not informing her of that particular fact, but since she was as happy as a clam now with Axel, she didn't beat him up with it too often.

"Give me my great-grandson," Squire told Sloan, and he was happy enough to push aside the memories as he detached the kid's fingers from his hair to set him on the floor. The kid immediately bulleted toward the gray-haired man, who scooped him up and blew a raspberry against his neck. Aidan's laughter filled the spacious room and immediately, young cousins began appearing, clamoring for similar treatment from the old man.

"I thought he was bad with his grandchildren," Tristan commented, leaving his spot that was no longer peaceful at all to follow Sloan back up the stairs. "He's twice as bad with his great-grandkids. The man was hell on us when we were growing up, but given the chance, he'll spoil the daylights out of them."

Sloan wondered if Abby's grandfather had been similarly inclined, or if her grandparents had been stricter because they'd taken on a parental role.

They made it to the top of the stairs and turned into the kitchen. The enormous table there was covered with a dozen desserts in varying stages of demolition, sidetracking both of them. Tristan studied his choices while Sloan helped himself to a hefty wedge of the chocolate cake he knew his sister had brought. It was the same cake his mother used to make for their birthdays when they were kids.

The cake was incredible. The memories that came with it weren't.

"Max sending you to that conference coming up in Cheyenne?"

Max had tried working on him to attend, but he couldn't see the point. Not when he wasn't even sure he was going to be around in a few months. "Dawson and Ruiz are going."

His sister entered the kitchen. "There you are." She was carrying Hank on her hip.

"Wasn't exactly hiding," he pointed out and watched the way his nephew eyed the cake on his fork. He knew better than to give the boy any, though. He'd made that mistake once already and quickly learned that Tara didn't want him having anything sugary until he was older.

Not that Hank the Tank was looking particularly deprived. The kid wasn't a year old yet, but he was already showing signs that he'd inherited the Clay genes when it came to size. He sure hadn't gotten his height from his petite mama. Tara was nearly a foot shorter than Sloan, and he and her husband were pretty much eye to eye.

"This is the first time I've had a chance to talk to you," she returned.

"Could've come talk to me earlier instead of sending your husband."

Tara's brown eyes flashed. "I didn't *send* Axel to do anything! As if the man ever does something he doesn't choose to do in the first place." Tristan made a noise and buried his attention in his pecan pie as he escaped. So much for the big-shot secret agent.

Sloan wished he could follow. He pushed his fork into the cake again and ignored the hopeful gleam in Hank's eyes. "He'd take a bullet for you."

She rubbed her cheek against Hank's bald head. "You're the one who took a bullet," she reminded him.

A graze. And it had been more than two years ago. She'd been pregnant with Aidan and on the verge of marrying Axel.

"But he has walked through fire for me," she allowed. "Literally."

"Which was my fault, too."

She shook her head. "I've never blamed you for what happened at the church that day when Maria's brother set that fire. He wanted to get back at you for her death by getting to me. He was insane with grief."

"You have more pity for him than I do." And more pity than the courts had. The lunatic had been convicted and would be locked away for a good long time.

"It's all water under the bridge, anyway," she dismissed. "If you really want a fresh start, don't you think that should include letting go of the past?"

He wished he could give her the answers she wanted to hear. "I don't want to promise something I'm not sure I can deliver."

She studied him for a moment. "Would you go back to the ATF if you could?"

He let out a humorless laugh. "Goob, they don't *want* me back." They'd made that plain enough when he'd been fired after the Deuce's trial had finally ended. They hadn't taken kindly to him drawing in anyone from Hollins-Winword to protect Maria or Tara. They'd told him it had shown a strong lack of faith in his own agency and conveniently ignored the fact that they hadn't been willing to provide any sort of protection themselves.

"But if you *could?*"

Would he? Nearly his entire adult life had been wrapped up in his ATF career. "I don't know. Maybe. Probably." He shook his head. "I don't know."

"Well," she said after a moment, "that's not what I wanted to talk to you about, anyway." She shifted Hank onto her other hip. "What's this I hear about you and your new neighbor? She's the new school nurse, right?"

He stared. "What do you know about her?"

"*She* was your mysterious plan last night, wasn't she?"

"She, who?" Max and his wife, Sarah, chose that moment to wander into the kitchen, and her blue gaze bounced from Sloan to Tara and back again. "Pretty little Abby Marcum?"

Sloan eyed his boss, but Max just shrugged. "Don't look at me. I might be the sheriff, but I don't know anything."

Sarah poked him in the side, and he jerked away, grinning. Then he frowned. "No more pecan pie?"

"Tristan finished it off."

"Figures." He took the last slice of chocolate cake. "This'll do just as well."

"Even after all these years together I do *not* know how you can eat the way you do and never gain a pound," Sarah complained. "You had a piece of Gloria's cheesecake an hour ago."

Max swatted her lightly on the butt. "My wife keeps me well exercised."

She rolled her eyes. "Here I thought you were going to help me get started on some of these dishes. Go on, then. Go back to your football game. I know that's what you really want to do."

"Always figure it's smart to get while the gettin's good." Max looked at Sloan. "You coming? Half time's over."

Sloan finished off his cake in a single bite and tossed the paper plate in the trash. "Just like Mom's," he told his twin, and then he did what any smart man would do and escaped while the escaping was good.

The house was cold again when Abby waked early the next morning. She pulled on a thick sweatshirt over her flannel pajamas and checked on Dillon, who was still sound asleep, before starting a pot of coffee. With the water gurgling and the scent of coffee beginning to fill the kitchen, she pushed her feet into her boots and let herself quietly out the door. She didn't like having to take more wood from Sloan's pile, but they'd burned through the last of what she had during the night, and she didn't want Dillon getting up to such a cold house.

Deputy Frosty's fat belly was just as fat as it had been the day before, but the striped scarf had fallen onto the ground. She stopped long enough to wind it around the snowman's neck, making sure the cardboard badge pinned to the knit was visible. Dillon had spent considerable time making the thing, and he'd certainly want to see it there today.

When she was finished, she balled her cold hands in the pockets of her sweatshirt and hurried across the yard.

"You're an early riser."

She nearly jumped out of her skin at the sound of Sloan's voice. The sky was gray and heavy, but it was still light enough to see him standing on his front porch.

And it was more than a little alarming the way pleasure engulfed her at the sight of him. Particularly considering the way he'd bolted the day before, after Pam Rasmussen had come by.

"So are you." Her voice sounded breathless but she couldn't help it. Seeing him made her feel breathless. "You're looking very official." He was coatless, too. But whereas she'd been caught in her flannel jammies and an oversize sweatshirt, he looked downright glorious in his uniform. He wore sharply creased khaki-colored pants with a dark green, long-sleeved shirt and black tie, complete with badge pinned to his insanely wide chest. She also noticed that, with a collared shirt, there was no hint that he had that intriguing tattoo that started on his neck and dipped beneath his clothing. "On duty today?" She cringed since it was pretty unlikely he would wear his uniform if he weren't.

"In a while." He lifted the mug he was holding. "Want some coffee?"

Even though she had her own pot brewing, she very nearly nodded. She pushed her fists deeper into her pockets, hoping to stretch the sweatshirt a little lower over her stupid pajama pants. "No, thanks. I was just going to grab some more wood. Dillon's still sleeping."

He straightened away from the post he'd been leaning against, set his mug on the rail and came down the steps toward her.

Her ability to breathe normally evaporated entirely.

All she could think of was the way he'd kissed her.

And the way he'd bolted.

Admittedly, he *had* been headed for a family dinner, but it still had felt as if he couldn't wait to escape.

He kept going when he reached her, though, angling toward the back of the house. "Half expected to see another snowman keeping Frosty company in your front yard."

She skipped to catch up with him and wished again that she'd taken the time to change into jeans. "If we get more snow out of those clouds, I expect he'll have company soon enough." She pulled one hand out of her pocket to tuck her hair behind her ear, only to realize she hadn't taken the time to brush her hair yet, either.

Lovely. Plaid pajamas, morning breath and a rat's nest of hair.

She ducked her chin into the collar of her sweatshirt and twitched the hood up over her hair.

"Cold?"

She smiled and shrugged, even though she was sure he was the cause of her shivering rather than the cold morning.

When they reached the back of the house, she quickly gathered several pieces of firewood. When he started to help her, she protested. "You're going to get your shirt dirty."

"Sweetheart, I've gotten worse things on my uniform before than a few wood slivers."

Sweetheart.

She shivered again and headed back around the side of the house, crossing diagonally to her front door.

Sloan followed her inside, and they stacked the wood next to the fireplace. "Looks like you did some more unpacking. Are they your grandparents?"

She glanced at the framed photographs he'd noticed on the mantel. "Yes."

"This you?" He tapped one in particular of Abby and her grandparents.

"We were pheasant hunting." She added a split log to the fire and jabbed the embers before adjusting the screen.

"How old were you?"

She didn't have to look at the photo to remind herself. "Seventeen." She and her grandfather had gone out hunting only one more time after that. It hadn't been the same without her grandmother coming along, but she hadn't been healthy enough at that point to accompany them.

"You look about thirteen."

And even more wet behind the ears, no doubt.

She pressed her hands against her flannel-covered thighs and straightened. "Maybe so," she said, "but he taught me to shoot almost as well as he could." She headed into the kitchen.

"You like hunting?"

"I liked going out with my grandparents. Without them?" She shrugged and filled a coffee cup. "I can't really see myself going out again. I don't think I have the heart for it." She took a sip, watching him over the brim of the cup. Not even the width of the living room was enough to dim the sheer wattage of him. "I'll get enough wood today to replace what I've used."

"I told you not to worry about that." He leaned on the breakfast counter. "Every time you talk about your grandparents, you look sad."

She started to tuck her hair behind her ear again, ran into that rat's nest of tangles and opened an overhead cabinet instead, pulling out the cardboard container of oatmeal to occupy herself. "I miss them. The worst thing about leaving Braden is not being able to visit my grandmother every day."

"It isn't that far away."

She smiled a little. "That's exactly what I keep telling Dillon." She realized they were in the same positions they'd been in when he'd kissed her and felt blood rushing into her face. She snatched up her coffee and took such a hasty drink that she almost gasped. "Aren't you on duty soon?" she asked abruptly.

His smile widened a little as if he knew exactly how he affected her. But he straightened and headed toward the door. She couldn't seem to help herself from following him out onto the porch. But the sudden shrieking of her name from inside the house had her racing right back inside, Sloan hard on her heels.

She met Dillon in the hallway, where he collided with her and grabbed on to her as though the world was ending.

Another nightmare.

Her heart squeezing, she sank down to the floor and pulled him right onto her lap. "I'm here, honey. Right here."

"I couldn't find you," he sobbed. "I looked everywhere, but—"

"Shh." She smoothed his hair back from his sweaty face and kissed his forehead. "I'm here, and I'm not going anywhere."

The hairs on the back of Sloan's neck slowly settled as he watched Abby sit there, comforting the boy.

"It was just a bad dream," he heard her say in a soothing voice. "And it's all gone, but I'm still here." She pressed her cheek to the top of the boy's head, her glossy brown hair blending with Dillon's.

He knew he should leave them to their privacy.

But walking out when the kid was so upset went against every grain in his body. He took a cautious step forward, and Abby focused on him.

"Look who else is here," she murmured to Dillon. "Deputy McCray came to say good morning to you."

It wasn't true, but Sloan didn't care. Particularly when the little boy peered around Abby at him. "You did?"

He took another step closer and crouched down. "I also wanted to say that you did a great job making Frosty's badge out there."

"It's not like yours, though."

Sloan unfastened his badge and held it up. "I think it was pretty close."

Dillon didn't unlatch himself from Abby, but he sat up a little straighter. "Abby helped me cut out the star."

"You drew the star first," Abby said.

She was watching him as closely as Dillon was, and Sloan wasn't sure whose gaze unnerved him more. "Do you want to wear it for a minute?"

Dillon's eyes went as wide as saucers. "Can I?"

Sloan knew Max well enough to know his boss wasn't going to sweat him being a little late for his shift. Not considering the situation. "You bet." He attached the badge to the boy's dinosaur-print pajama shirt. "How does it feel?"

Dillon scrambled to his feet and darted into the bathroom that opened onto the hall. Sloan could see him stretching as high as he could to see himself in the mirror over the sink.

Abby gave Sloan a grateful smile and pushed to her feet, as well. She followed Dillon into the small bathroom and lifted him higher. "Pretty cool, huh?"

"The coolest," Dillon breathed. He wriggled, and Abby set him back on his feet. He came back out into the hallway, his thin chest puffed out. "When I'm big, I'm gonna be a deputy, too."

Abby's pretty eyes met Sloan's. "Thank you," she mouthed silently.

Then she touched Dillon's shoulder. "Deputy McCray

probably needs his badge back now, Dillon, so he can go to work."

"Okay." But before Sloan could unfasten the badge, the kid was already doing it, the tip of his tongue sticking out the corner of his mouth as he looked down to see what he was doing. When he'd unpinned it, he held the badge out on his flattened palm. "Watch your back out there," he said solemnly.

Sloan managed not to smile.

Abby wasn't so successful. The smile that her lips seemed created to wear was back on her face.

He took the badge and pinned it in place. He gave a quick salute and headed toward the front door.

"He's a real White Hat," he heard Dillon whisper behind him. "Isn't he?"

Sloan didn't wait to hear Abby's answer as he let himself out through the front door. Whatever the White Hats were that the kid was talking about, Sloan knew that he'd never worn one.

White Hats were for the good guys.

They weren't for the guys who'd only ever hurt the ones who least deserved it.

Chapter Five

Even though Sloan had told her not to worry about it, when Abby and Dillon went out later that afternoon and visited the big-box Shop-World on the far side of town, she added a few extra bags of firewood to their shopping cart. When they got back to the house and unloaded their purchases, she carted the bags to the rear of his house, pulled off the plastic and stacked the wood neatly on top of his pile.

By then, it had started snowing again, and she and Dillon spent the rest of the afternoon inside. They unpacked the last few boxes, played a game of 'White Hats' and baked a batch of chocolate cookies while the repairman she'd called fixed the furnace. And even though they were busy pretty much all day long, Abby was hyperaware that the SUV with Sheriff on the side didn't reappear in the driveway next door all day. It wasn't there when she caved to Dillon's constant begging and let him take a covered plate of the cookies to leave on Sloan's front porch. It wasn't there, even after she'd read a story to Dillon and tucked him into bed, and it wasn't there when she hustled him out of the house the next morning for his first day at his new school. *Their* new school.

Mercifully, she didn't have any extra time to think about the handsome deputy as Principal Gage gave her a tour of the school and she settled into the office that was now hers. She checked supplies, read through the files of the students who had continuing health-care needs and by lunchtime had seen a half-dozen children for everything from an earache to a girl having her first period. She was so busy, in fact, that she ate her peanut butter and jelly sandwich in her office and didn't leave it at all until she went with the rest of the teachers and administration to attend the assembly being held in the gymnasium.

There, she stood in the back of the room while the students noisily claimed their patches of gym floor and sat down. They were arranged by classes with the youngest in front and the oldest in back, and Abby didn't even realize how nervous she was for Dillon until she spotted him sitting cross-legged next to a little blond-haired girl who, judging by the way she was chattering away, didn't seem too put off by Dillon's apparent silence.

Then the genial principal moved to the front of the room, efficiently gathering the children's attention while the teachers began moving to the back of the room where a few rows of folding chairs were set up.

"Come on." Dee Crowder, one of the first teachers Abby had met that morning, nudged Abby along the row of seats. She taught third grade and was short like Abby with wildly curly blond hair and an infectious smile that reminded her of Delia's. "There's room for you to sit, too."

So Abby scooted along the row of chairs to the end and dutifully sat down. "How often are there assemblies?"

Dee shrugged and pulled a tube of lip gloss from the pocket of her red sweater. "Couple times a month. They don't always have all the grades at once, though. Today it's just because of the presentation."

Abby knew that safety and drug-abuse prevention were the topics this afternoon. While she certainly supported the cause, she hoped the assembly wouldn't drag on too long. She still had a stack of student files to get through.

"I don't know why I thought moving to one of the condos out near Shop-World would come with better pickings where men are concerned," Dee whispered. She bumped her shoulder against Abby's. "You buy the old Downing place that's been empty for a year and basically hit the lottery."

Abby dragged her thoughts from the unread files waiting for her to the teacher next to her. "Sorry?"

"I'm stuck in a lease, living between newlyweds on one side and a lady who has four cats on the other, and you move in next door to the hottest guy in town."

She realized that Dee's avid gaze was glued to the front of the gymnasium and followed it.

There stood Sloan, alongside Sheriff Scalise and two other officers.

And even though she was sitting in the back of a very crowded gymnasium, when his attention traveled across the audience, it seemed as if his gaze honed right in on her.

She moistened her lips and shifted in her seat.

The sheriff had taken over the microphone at the podium after the principal finished his spiel about home emergency plans, but she barely heard a word of what he said.

Sloan looked as magnificent in his uniform now as he had the morning before.

Dee leaned close again, her whisper barely audible. "You might know he'd be good-looking. He's not a Clay, but his sister married one, and there's not a dud in the bunch."

Abby had grown up in Braden, but anyone who lived in the state had heard of the Clay family. There was the cattle ranch they owned, the Double-C, which was one of the largest in the state. There was Cee-Vid, the company that put out games like 'White Hats.' It, too, was run by one of the Clays and was located right there in Weaver. There was also the hospital—the only one in the region. From the stories her grandparents had told, building it had come about mostly because of the Clays' efforts.

"Even Sheriff Scalise fits the mold," Dee was saying. "He married Sarah Clay."

Abby had met Sarah that morning. She was the other third-grade teacher. And Dee had a point. Sheriff Scalise definitely qualified as tall, dark and handsome. But there was nothing about the married father of three that made Abby's mouth run dry.

Unlike his newest deputy.

Sloan and one of the other deputies—a slender woman with dark blond hair—had begun moving along the rows of students and were handing out stacks of flyers.

"Half of those flyers are going to end up as paper airplanes," Dee whispered. "Mark my words."

"What are they about?"

As the deputies went row to row, the noise level in the cavernous room was rising, and Dee didn't bother to keep her voice down. "They have a drawing contest every year for their drug-abuse resistance program. The winners from each grade get to do a ride-along in a car with an on-duty officer—all geared appropriately toward their level, of course—and then from those drawings, they'll choose a final winner. The drawings will be used on all the flyers and brochures about the program for the next year." She suddenly popped out of her seat. "Calvin Pierce." Her voice, surprisingly loud for someone so small, rang out across the room. "That shoe belongs on your foot, not on your neighbor's head."

Abby saw a towheaded little boy near Dillon sink guiltily onto his bottom and shove his foot back into his shoe.

Dee sighed and sat back down herself. "It's a popular program with the kids," she went on as if there'd been no interruption whatsoever. "And anything that keeps the message going about saying no is a good thing as far as I'm concerned. It was Joe's—Principal Gage's—idea. They are trying to come up with something similar that would be just as popular at the junior-high and high-school levels. But they're a tougher audience." She sighed a little then crossed her legs and looked at Abby. "Don't you think he's hot? You know," she prompted when Abby hesitated. "Your neighbor."

For a moment, Abby had thought the other woman meant Principal Gage. "I don't know Deputy McCray all that well." She just knew what his lips tasted like. How he smelled. How his smile was too long in coming…

"That's not what I hear."

Abby started. "Hear from whom?"

"You're from Braden, right?" Dee barely waited for Abby to nod. "Then you know how word gets around."

"Not always an accurate word, though." She felt flustered right down to her bones, and it wasn't helped by the fact that Sloan had reached the back of the room where they were sitting.

"Ladies." He handed Abby, who was at the end of the

row, the rest of the flyers he'd been holding, and his fingers brushed against hers.

"Deputy McCray." Dee smiled brilliantly and took the stack, save one sheet, out of Abby's nerveless grasp. She kept a few for herself before passing them along to the teacher beside her. "It's so nice to see you taking part today."

Sloan barely glanced at the curly-haired teacher as he gave a noncommittal smile. "Part of the job."

He did, however, do more than glance at Abby, and she could have melted into her metal folding seat when his smile seemed to warm for her alone. "Thanks for the cookies," he told her. "You make them yourself?"

Much too aware of Dee's attention, Abby lifted her shoulders. "Dillon thought you needed some." It was only half the truth.

Her little brother *had* thought Sloan needed some since they'd used his store-bought cookies for both the snowman's eyes and Dillon's stomach. But while she'd mixed up the chocolaty dough, Abby hadn't been able to forget that her grandmother always claimed she'd caught Abby's grandfather with that very same recipe. Since they'd married only a month after a young Minerva had offered an equally young Thomas one of her cookies at a church bake sale, and had stayed married for the rest of their lives, Abby figured the story had some merit.

"Then I'll have to thank Dillon, too." He began making his way back up to the front of the room where the principal was making an effort to quiet the crowd.

Dee bumped her shoulder again. "Make cookies for everyone you barely know? Your other neighbors, too?"

The woman was grinning with such good cheer that Abby couldn't help but like her. "My other neighbor has been out of town," she said blithely. "But, yes, I'll have a plate for him." She'd have to make another batch, but that was moot.

Dee laughed soundlessly and turned her attention back to the principal.

Soon after, the gymnasium was once again a madhouse as the students were dismissed back to their classrooms. Abby slowly folded her chair and stacked it against the rest. She knew she was lingering, watching Sloan as he stood at the front of the room talking with the principal and the sheriff.

But he didn't look her way again, and rather than being the last person to leave, she made her way back to her office and the files awaiting her. She didn't have a chance to finish studying them, though, because a boy came in with a bloody nose, and then she needed to see several students at the junior high next door to administer their regular medications.

When she collected Dillon at the end of the day, he had a stack of work sheets clutched in his hand that he was supposed to finish at home, and she had a stack of district policies to read. "We both have homework," she told him as they set off for the short walk home. "What do you have to work on there?"

He pushed the papers into his backpack then hitched it over his shoulders. "Spelling. And we gotta turn in a report about our 'mergency plan at home."

Two things he would fly through, she knew. Dillon was all about what to do in an emergency. She'd already shown him how to open all the windows in the house in case there was a fire and they couldn't get out the front door. "What about the drawing contest the sheriff talked about? Do you want to enter?"

He ducked his chin. He took her hand as they crossed

the street that had gone quiet again after the last of the students had departed. "Dunno."

Surprised, she looked down at him. "You love to draw. Why not?"

"Calvin says only weenies enter the contest."

Abby squelched the first response that came to her mind where Calvin was concerned. "Who is Calvin?"

"Calvin Pierce," he muttered, his chin even deeper in his coat.

The same towheaded boy that Dee had called out during the assembly. "Calvin is in your class?" The growing school had two classes each for most grades.

Dillon nodded. They followed the sidewalk around the corner onto their street. "I gotta sit at the same table as him." He sounded morose. "In the *front* row."

"Well, maybe you won't be in the front row all the time," she said encouragingly. "And you shouldn't listen to nonsense from any of the other kids about entering a contest that I know you must be interested in. Don't you want a chance to see what it's like to be a deputy like Deputy Mc-Cray? You would get to tour the sheriff's office and ride in one of their official vehicles."

"I prob'ly wouldn't win anyway." He tugged his mitten-covered hand free of hers and hitched up the straps of his backpack again.

Abby hid a sigh. "You don't know that unless you try." She decided to drop the matter for now. "How did you like your teacher?"

"Ms. Normington's okay. She's got a goldfish on her desk."

"And the other kids in your class? Besides Calvin?"

"They're okay."

She chewed the inside of her lip and watched him as

they reached the edge of their yard. "Who was the girl you were sitting next to during the assembly?"

"Chloe."

"She looked pretty friendly." Talkative, at any rate, from what Abby had observed.

"She's at my table, too." He suddenly looked up at her. "Is Deputy McCray gonna be your boyfriend?"

She stopped in her tracks. A squiggle of something worked around inside her chest, messing with her breathing. "Of course not!"

He peered at her. "Wouldn't he be a good one?"

Thoughts of just how good Sloan might be in all sorts of roles swirled inside her head, nearly making her choke. "I have no idea," she managed to say with a reasonable amount of calm, all things considered. "Deputy McCray is a nice man who lives next door to us. That's all." She moistened her lips. "Why would you even ask that question?"

But he seemed to have lost interest in the subject just as quickly as he'd brought it up. He hitched his backpack up again and set off across the snow, stopping only long enough to reposition the snowman's sagging carrot nose. "Can we have skeddi for supper?"

"Sure," she said faintly and wished her own thoughts could be so easily switched.

What would Sloan be like as a *boyfriend?*

The term was almost laughable, because there was nothing boyish about him.

He was a man. All man.

And while she had no personal experience being *with* a man, her imagination where Sloan was concerned worked just fine.

Too fine.

Warmth flowed through her, making her feel a little weak.

She swallowed, glancing over at the two-storied house next door as she unlocked her front door and waited for Dillon to go inside. But when she saw the familiar SUV turning onto their street at the end of the block, she jumped as if she'd been caught doing something wicked and rushed inside after her little brother, closing the door harder than necessary.

"What's wrong?"

"Not a thing. The wind caught the door." She blamed the heat in her cheeks on the lie. "Why don't you sit at the counter to do your work sheets? I'll get you some milk and a cookie to hold you over until spaghetti. Okay?"

He nodded as he started unearthing himself from his coat. She left him to it and hurried into her bedroom, where she dumped her briefcase on her dresser and ignored her flushed reflection in the mirror as she pulled off her own coat and gloves. Then she exchanged her navy suit for jeans and a sweatshirt from nursing college and yanked her hair up into a clip on top of her head. The person looking back at her in the mirror now was the one she felt more familiar with than the RN who wore a suit and carried her grandfather's ancient leather briefcase.

She headed back out to the kitchen. Dillon was sitting at the breakfast counter, hunched over a work sheet with his pencil clenched in his fist. The tip of his tongue was caught in the corner of his mouth.

She smiled, resisted the urge to smack a kiss on his head and poured him the promised glass of milk. She set two of the chocolate cookies they'd baked together on a napkin beside his milk and began pulling together the makings for spaghetti sauce. When the doorbell rang a few minutes later, she didn't even have a chance to set down her knife before Dillon hopped off his perch. "I'll get it!"

It was so out of character for her usually shy brother

that she hated to caution him, but she still followed him. And then she went dry-mouthed all over again after Dillon pulled open the door to reveal Sloan standing there on the step.

When his eyes met hers, her stomach swooped and her riotous imagination went completely berserk. She was glad for Dillon's presence, because she could only imagine what the good townspeople of Weaver would have to say if the new school nurse tried to jump their deputy sheriff's bones right there on the front porch.

"We're having skeddi," her little brother announced, grabbing Sloan's hand and pulling him right inside. "You want to have some, too?" He shut the door hard, as if he could keep Sloan from leaving by that act alone.

Abby opened her mouth. Closed it again.

She knew she was blushing and there wasn't a darn thing she could do about it.

Sloan was still eyeing her, his expression amused—hopefully because of Dillon's enthusiasm and not because he could read her X-rated thoughts. He was holding the empty cookie plate. "He say that to every guy who comes to your door with plate in hand?"

She managed a smile. Very few guys had ever come to her door once they knew about Dillon. And none at all with an empty cookie plate from her. But she had no intention of telling him that or about anything else that was currently in her head. "You're welcome to join us for dinner. Spaghetti with marinara," she translated and gestured vaguely toward the kitchen. Her hand was shaking. "Although it's going to be a while."

"Abby makes her own skeddi sauce," Dillon said, sounding boastful. "She doesn't pour it out of a jar."

She'd never thought she'd be the center of a public-relations spin, much less one offered by a seven-year-old boy. "Your homework isn't going to get done by itself." She nudged him toward the breakfast counter.

"They give homework to second-graders?"

She looked back at Sloan and, with nothing to occupy her nervous hands, tucked her fingers in the back pockets of her jeans. "He had homework even in kindergarten."

"Only things I remember from kindergarten are graham crackers and nap time. Didn't matter which school, they were all the same." He touched her shoulder as he stepped around her to head into the kitchen with the empty plate.

All he'd done was touch her shoulder and she wanted to shiver. "You went to more than one school while you were in *kindergarten?*" She'd known the same kids from kindergarten right through high-school graduation.

He turned on the hot water and ran the perfectly clean plate under it. "Three." His voice sounded short, and he didn't look at her as he set the plate in the sink and turned toward Dillon.

Abby's breath came a little easier with his focus no longer on her. She poured olive oil into a pot and set it on the stove. Breathing might have been easier, but the man still occupied the kitchen with her, and the room had never felt smaller.

He picked up one of the papers spread across the counter, glanced at it and set it back down. "What're you going to draw for the contest at school, champ?"

"I dunno."

Abby hesitated, ready to jump in, but Sloan leaned on the counter until he was down at Dillon's height. "Figured you'd already have a lock on it."

Dillon didn't even look at Abby. "Really?"

"Sure," Sloan said easily, as if he'd dealt with inse-cure, wishful children every day. "You made that badge for Frosty and it was great."

She slowly scraped her diced onions and celery into the pot, holding her breath as she listened. Dillon's attitude toward the contest was considerably more positive with Sloan than it had been with her, and she didn't want to mess with progress.

"But I gotta draw more 'n a badge," her little brother was saying.

No mention whatsoever about Calvin Pierce and his weenie theory. She chewed the inside of her lip to keep a smile from forming.

"Says who?" Sloan challenged lightly. "You heard what Sheriff Scalise said, didn't you? If a badge means doing the right thing to you, then draw a badge." He lowered his voice a notch. "You think Abby has any more of those chocolate cookies hanging around?"

"Yup!" Dillon hopped off his chair again and dashed around the counter, dragging down the plastic container holding the cookies. "Deputy McCray says I can draw a badge for the contest," he told her in a loud whisper.

"I heard," she whispered back. It was almost impossible to keep from glancing at Sloan, but she managed.

While Dillon set the cookies on the counter and flipped off the lid, she reached in the cabinet and pulled out a squat crystal glass. She filled it with milk and set it in front of Sloan.

"Thanks." His long fingers slid around the glass.

She returned to the stove and stirred the softly sizzling contents with a wooden spoon. It was a much safer occupation than imagining how his fingers would feel sliding over *her*.

"Golly." Dillon drew out the exclamation. "Abby never lets us use Grandma's glasses."

"And you're still not using Grandma's glasses," she said, sending him a wry smile. Dillon had an entire selection of plastic glasses patterned with dinosaurs. "One day, they'll be yours, but only if they stay unbroken until then."

He wrinkled his nose. "I don't want no fancy glasses. They're for *girls*."

"Then someday you can give them to the girl you marry."

Looking even more horrified, he leaned over and made a loud retching sound.

Sloan's gaze caught hers, and she rolled her eyes. "Little boys," she dismissed, as if that explained it all.

"I'm not so ancient that I can't remember being one myself." His lips crooked and his gaze seemed to rove over her.

She went breathless all over again, her hand tightening spasmodically around the spoon's long handle. And when Sloan took a step closer, she froze altogether.

"Good thing he doesn't know all the things he has in store for him one day." He lowered his voice a notch, and his breath whispered against her temple. "Kid would be taking cold showers in the middle of the night like I've been doing since you moved next door."

Her jaw loosened as she stared at him.

Then the radio attached to his belt crackled noisily and she jumped. The spoon slid out of her fingers, falling into the pot.

He looked from her face to the stove as he spoke into the radio, responding to the gibberish that she couldn't begin to understand. In the span of seconds, he'd returned the radio to his belt. "Going to have to take a rain check on the spaghetti." He reached around her to fish the spoon out of the pot and set it aside. "Better be careful." His voice was low. "Don't want to burn yourself."

Then he turned out of the kitchen, fist-bumping Dillon on the way to the door.

She exhaled shakily.

His warning came too late.

She was already burning, and the cause of it had just walked out of her house.

Chapter Six

Sloan sat in the Pierces' shabby living room with Lorraine after Max took Bobby away in handcuffs.

There was no smell of fragrant cooking filling this house.

He'd left that behind at Abby's.

In fact, it seemed to Sloan that he'd left behind everything warm and comfortable at Abby's to spend the past four hours in a house that was cold and a helluva lot worse than *un*comfortable.

Even though he wanted to shake some sense into Lorraine, he didn't. She was the victim here no matter what she claimed to the contrary. She was too thin. More ragged than any female her age should ever have to be.

He remembered thinking the same thing about his mother when he was young. She hadn't been an abused wife, but she damn sure hadn't known what sort of life she'd be in for when she'd married Sloan's dad.

He blocked out the thoughts the way he always did and wished the counselor they'd called to come and talk with Lorraine would hurry up and get there.

"Lorraine." This was a close community. No point for *Mr.* and *Mrs.* when you were just as likely to sit next to the people you were serving and protecting at the local bar on Saturday night as in the church pew on Sunday morning. "You have more power than you think." He sat forward on the threadbare chair, wishing to hell that he could convince her and knowing just as well that he probably never would.

The Pierce home had been the first call he'd gone out on when he'd signed on with the sheriff's department, and not a month had passed since when he hadn't had to repeat the visit. Six months in Weaver. Six months of trying. Six months of failing.

"You don't have to keep taking this sort of thing from your husband," he continued. "You'll have support."

Lorraine looked away. Her arms were folded tightly across her thin chest. "Bobby takes care of me and Cal. And you and the sheriff got no right busting in here again just 'cause we got a couple of nosy neighbors."

He pinched the bridge of his nose. "The neighbors called because they were worried." He gestured at what had once been the front picture window but was now covered over with the large sheet of plywood that he'd had put up to keep out the cold. "*Somebody* threw that kitchen chair out that window." They'd found the chair stuck in a snowdrift glittering with broken glass. "It didn't happen by itself. We've got probable cause, Lorraine. We don't need for you to say Bobby's a danger to you when we can see it for ourselves."

She angled her bony jaw and looked away. "I told you Calvin was the one who threw the chair. That's why I sent him to his room."

Sloan grimaced. "Blaming it on your kid? That's a new low, Lorraine."

She blinked a few times. But she didn't recant.

He rose, feeling hemmed in by the depressing aura that filled the room. He didn't move too fast because moving at all seemed to make Lorraine even more nervous.

He wanted to shake her. But mostly, he just wanted to protect her. Get her to protect herself *and* that boy of hers she seemed willing to throw under the bus to save her husband's sorry hide. When he'd spoken with Calvin, the boy had been sullen and full of attitude. If he *had* tossed the chair through the window, he'd have bragged left and right about it. But Calvin had said nothing.

There was a small collection of photos in cheap picture frames hanging crookedly on the wall, and he studied them. No school pictures of Calvin. No family portraits. Just snapshots of Bobby, arm looped over the shoulders of one buddy or another. In all of them, the men were astride their Harleys. Like the Deuces, Bobby put more money into his ride than he did his home.

He blocked the memories again, staring restlessly up the narrow staircase leading to the second floor, where Calvin had been banished to his room by his mother. The counselor was coming as much for the boy's benefit as Lorraine's.

Again, Sloan wished that Dr. Templeton would hurry. When they'd called her, she'd been over in Braden dealing with an emergency there, but she'd promised to be there as soon as she could.

"Bobby loves me, you know."

"Maybe he does, Lorraine—" a twisted version of it, in Sloan's estimation "—but you shouldn't have to go around being afraid in your own home of someone who loves you."

The doorbell rang then, and since he was close he answered the door himself and let in Dr. Templeton. She apologized for being so long as she unwound her knit scarf and peeled off her gloves. The doctor was about Sloan's age, though she looked a lot younger, and if she felt the same stifling depressiveness inside the Pierce home that he did, she hid it well. She sat down next to Lorraine as if they were two girlfriends getting together to dish about their day.

Sloan didn't care what her approach was as long as it worked.

With no official reason to remain, he left them to it and returned to the office, wrote up his report and headed back home.

It was getting late, and golden light was shining from the front window of Abby's house when he pulled into his driveway next door. If he went over and knocked on her door, he knew that she'd let him in. That her pretty eyes would be soft, and her lips would curve into a genuine smile.

And they'd taste sweeter than anything he'd tasted in a long, long while.

She was a lot more of a mother to Dillon than just a sister. Just as much a mother, in fact, as Lorraine was to Calvin. But there was no other comparison he could draw between them. Sloan, though, could have been looking at himself in those pictures on Lorraine's wall.

He'd helped take down the Deuces. He'd infiltrated them with the sole purpose of doing so. He'd befriended their leader, Johnny Diablo, until the man thought of him like a real brother. He'd prepped for his cover for more than a year then rode with them for more than three. And it had been another two after that before the case ever made it to court. Two years when he'd remained underground still, just to keep the Deuces from finding him.

Nearly his entire adult life had been consumed by the deadly gang.

But even now, after it was all said and done, Sloan wasn't sure how much of himself he'd left behind with them.

He sat there for a long while looking at the golden glow spreading over the front of Abby's yard where the snowman stood sentry. He sat there until the still engine no longer ticked and the truck's interior went cold.

Then he climbed out, feeling stiff and older than his years, and went inside his own dark house.

"How's life with Deputy Hottie?"

Abby looked up from the first-aid supplies she was inventorying to see Dee Crowder strolling into her office. There was no point pretending she didn't know who the teacher meant.

Nor was there any point in pretending that Sloan hadn't been avoiding her. It had been an entire week since he'd returned the cookie plate. A week since he'd implied that she'd been the cause of some sleepless nights for him.

He did more than imply it.

She ignored the voice inside her head and closed the metal supply cabinet. "I told you. We're just neighbors." She couldn't even say they were neighbors who flirted. He may have made that comment, but he hadn't so much as glanced toward their house during his comings and goings since then.

She knew this because she'd spent a lot of her time surreptitiously watching for *him*.

Dee set a foam cup on Abby's desk. "Fresh coffee from the teacher's lounge." She leaned her hip on the corner of the desk. It was the middle of the afternoon, and she'd made a habit of stopping by Abby's office during her prep period.

Abby had quickly realized that Dee's excuse for dropping by with coffee was just as much an excuse to smile and wave at the principal, whose office was next door to hers.

The curly-haired teacher had it bad for Principal Gage but hid it behind impish smiles and a wolf whistle for any male beyond the age of consent.

Abby pulled out her squeaky desk chair and sat down, gratefully taking a sip of the coffee. She grimaced, though, and looked up at Dee. "This is *fresh?*" The most she could say about it was that it was hot.

"Made it myself." Then Dee grinned. "Of course, the coffee maker in there probably hasn't been cleaned in a decade. A bunch of us spinsters get together once a month for Friday-night poker. If you're really just *neighbors* with Deputy McCray, then I guess you're almost one of us. Tomorrow night at my place. Want to come?"

"I would," Abby said truthfully. "But I can't leave Dillon."

"I can recommend a half-dozen sitters," Dee coaxed.

Abby didn't doubt her. The other woman seemed to know every name in town. "I still wouldn't want to leave him. He's—" how could she describe her brother? "—still settling in here." Dillon was the only one that Sloan didn't seem to be avoiding. He'd done more than share the time of day with her little brother; he'd even helped Dillon make another snowman to keep Deputy Frosty company. But the second that Abby had gone out to join them, Sloan had made an excuse to leave.

Dee looked thoughtful for a moment. "How 'bout if we meet at your place instead?" Then she grinned again. "Or is that too pushy of me?"

It was, but Abby could only laugh. Dee's good humor had that effect. And maybe with the distraction of a girls' night—even a girls' night *in*—Abby wouldn't dwell so much on Sloan. "What time?"

"Seven. You got a good table, or should we pack a few card tables and folding chairs?"

"Chairs, I guess," she started. "But what else—?"

Dee waved her hand, hopping off the desk. "Nothing else. All the necessities will come to *you*." She suddenly tugged a curl out of her face and hurried into the corridor. "Hi, there, Principal Gage," she greeted.

Abby sank her teeth into her lip, trying not to giggle.

But really, was she any different than Dee? Dreaming about a man who didn't seem to be all that interested after all?

Joe barely looked at Dee and turned into Abby's office instead. The serious look on his face ended any desire whatsoever that she had to giggle. "Ms. Marcum, would you mind coming into my office?"

Alarm climbed up into her throat. She nodded and quickly stepped around her desk and followed him. Behind the man's back, Dee caught her gaze, lifting her eyebrows, and Abby shrugged a little helplessly.

"Call me," the other woman mouthed.

Abby nodded and turned into the school's main office. Joe's secretary, Viola Timms, was sitting at her desk. She looked thin-lipped and humorless, but since that was the way she always looked as she guarded the doorway to her boss's office, Abby couldn't take any clue from her. Feeling as if she'd done something wrong, and not knowing what, she passed by the older woman and went through the doorway.

Then she stopped short.

Dillon was sitting in the chair in front of Joe's wide

desk, hunched over and looking too small. "Dillon?" She hurried toward him and gasped when he turned to face her. He'd obviously been hit in the face. His nose and eye were swollen. She crouched next to him, lifting his chin with her fingers. "Who did this to you?"

"Nobody," Dillon mumbled. "Can't we just go home now?"

Abby gaped at her little brother. "Dillon!"

Joe closed his office door and moved around to lean against the front of his desk. "Mr. Rasmussen found him in the boys' room," he told Abby. "Dillon." His voice went a shade sterner. "I can tell your sister or you can."

More alarmed than ever, she squeezed Dillon's cold hands. Rob Rasmussen was one of the sixth-grade teachers. "What happened, honey?" This was the hour that his class was supposed to be in chorus.

Dillon flicked a gaze at the principal then ducked his chin again. "Was in a fight," he said, almost inaudibly.

Abby absorbed that. Dillon never acted out. In Braden, he'd been so introverted that she'd worried about him. Since coming to Weaver, though, he'd started to come out of his shell.

Mostly with Sloan.

"Who were you fighting with?"

His lips clamped shut, and she looked up at Joe.

"Calvin Pierce," he provided.

She looked back at her little brother. "Honey, if he's picking on you, you need to tell me about it!"

Joe stirred at that. "Dillon, I want you to go sit by Mrs. Timms's desk and wait for your sister while we talk."

Without looking at her, Dillon slid off the chair and shuffled out of the office, dragging his coat and backpack behind him. Joe closed the door after him.

"I don't know what to say." Abby felt bewildered and

knew it sounded in her voice. "Dillon doesn't like sitting at the same table with Calvin in class, but I had no idea it was this bad between them."

"Calvin is a challenge," Joe said quietly. "I won't deny that. But I'm not sure he was the one who started the fight. Not this time."

"What do you mean?"

"Mr. Rasmussen saw Dillon throw the first punch."

She stared. "I don't believe it. That's just not like him."

"And it is entirely like Calvin," Joe agreed. "But it's not like Rob to get the details wrong." He gave her a regretful look. "Dillon won't tell me what instigated the scuffle."

"Did Calvin?"

His lips tightened a little. "Calvin actually claims he was the one who started it," he allowed. But he still shook his head. "Forgive the expression, but he's protecting his reputation as a hard-ass."

"He's *seven!*"

"Eight, actually. And he comes from a family I wouldn't wish on my worst enemy. Look, Abby. I'm not trying to say Calvin is a saint. There've been more than a few times when he's been at fault in similar situations, and maybe he is this time, as well. But I've been doing this job for a long time. I recognize that neither of those boys is being truthful with me, and I'm going to trust that my teacher is accurately describing what he saw. Dillon and Calvin *were* fighting. And that's not allowed. So I'm suspending them both until Monday."

Abby swallowed. Suspended. She'd never been suspended in her life. And now, in the second grade, Dillon already had been.

"It's only for a day," he added, sounding sympathetic. "And I know you're new in town, so you'll probably need to take the day off to stay home with him, as well. I don't want you to worry about this affecting your position here or anything. I'll call in a backup for you here for the rest of today and tomorrow."

She hadn't even gotten so far as to think about that. "I appreciate it. Did you tell Dillon he's been suspended?"

"Yes."

She closed her eyes for a moment, sending a silent apology to her grandparents for the rotten job she was apparently doing. Then she blew out a breath and stood. "I'm sorry about all this," she told Joe.

He accompanied her to the door and opened it for her. "It happens, Abby. Talk to Dillon. Find out why. Let's try to keep it from happening again." He sounded more encouraging than judgmental, and Abby could see a little more clearly why Dee was so taken with him.

With Dillon in tow, she stopped at her office, collected her things and locked up. Then they headed outside and began walking home.

It was quiet and felt strange without the usual end-of-day chaos. And it seemed entirely fitting when she realized it was starting to snow again. "Principal Gage said you were the one who started the fight," she finally said. "You want to tell me why?"

Dillon walked on, silently.

She tried another tack. "Was Calvin making fun of you entering the sheriff's contest?" Dillon had been drawing badges for a week now. They were pinned up all over the walls of his bedroom.

But Dillon just shook his head.

"Honey, I wish you'd tell me why it happened. I'm going to have to come up with some sort of punishment, and if I knew why, maybe it would help."

He looked at her as though he wanted to argue. But still he said nothing.

She exhaled. "I guess I'll have to take away my per-mission for that field trip next week." The second- and third-grade classes were going to tour Cee-Vid, and Dil-lon had talked of little else since he'd brought home the permission slip.

"No! That's where they make 'White Hats'!"

"I know. So tell me *why* you were fighting."

His mouth clamped shut. He pulled up the hood of his jacket and kept walking.

Abby dashed a snowflake from her face and kept walk-ing, too. She was so frustrated, worried and focused on Dillon that she didn't even notice at first the sound of an engine until Dillon stopped on the sidewalk and looked.

Sloan was pulling up beside them in his SUV. The pas-senger window rolled down, and he looked across at them. "You two look like you're in need of a ride. You heading home?"

It was pointless to deny it, though Abby was tempted. He just looked so darned *good.* And she felt so darned miserable.

Without a word, she pulled open the door, gesturing for Dillon to get in. He scrambled up into the front seat. She closed the door and got in the back, which was separated from the front by a see-through grille. She shuddered a little. Dillon was getting a taste of a ride-along regardless of the drawing contest, but Abby wasn't enjoying it one little bit. She felt like some sort of criminal.

Maybe her crime was moving her brother from every-thing he knew in Braden. If they'd stayed, none of this would be happening.

"You going home sick or something?" Sloan asked Dil-lon. "Your face looks swollen."

"Nuh-uh."

"Dillon's face looks swollen because he got punched,"

Abby said bluntly. "He was fighting and got suspended. *That* is why we're going home."

Sloan looked over his shoulder at her. He looked as poleaxed as she felt.

She turned away and stared out the window. At least he seemed to genuinely care about Dillon. Not that she knew him well enough to know anything for sure.

"Why were you fighting, bud?"

Good luck, she thought. That was the million-dollar question.

"'Cause Calvin Pierce called me a liar."

She snapped forward on the seat when Dillon answered as if he'd only been waiting to be asked. "What?" She latched her fingertips through the cold metal grille. "*Now* you're in the mood to explain?"

Sloan shot her a look through the mirror.

She pressed her lips together and subsided.

"What did he say you were lying about?" Sloan asked calmly.

It was probably easy for him to be calm. Dillon was an ordinarily shy seven-year-old. Sloan was used to dealing with a treacherous motorcycle gang full of murderers and gun runners.

"I told him I wore a real deputy badge, and he said I didn't. That I was a liar *and* a weenie."

"Oh, Dillon," Abby said, sighing. She sat forward and started to put her fingertips on the grille again but stopped just in time. "It doesn't matter what someone else says to you. You can't start a fight because of it."

"He said I was a liar," Dillon repeated. His agitated voice rose. "I never been a *liar*. That's what Black Hats do!"

"Take it easy, bud," Sloan said. He turned onto their street and a moment later was parking in his driveway.

"Let's go inside and you can tell us about it." He turned off the engine, and he and Dillon opened their front doors to get out. Abby tried, too, but the handle on her door did absolutely nothing, and she had to wait for Sloan to come around and open it for her.

"Back doors don't open from the inside," he pointed out needlessly.

She quickly climbed out, feeling no small amount of relief. "Thanks for the ride," she told him. "But I think I've got it from here on out." Without looking at him again, she grabbed Dillon's hand and headed across the yard. "You and I are going to have a little talk," she warned when they reached their front steps.

"Abby. Wait."

She unlocked the door and nudged Dillon inside before she turned and faced Sloan.

He'd followed them across the yard. Snowflakes glittered in his hair, and he was so freaking beautiful that it was almost painful to look at him.

"This isn't your problem," she told him huskily.

"It is if it all started because I let him wear my badge for a few minutes." He looked genuinely pained.

"It doesn't matter if Dillon did or didn't wear your badge. He's old enough to know right from wrong. And he knows that fighting is wrong."

"It's not always wrong."

She exhaled roughly and tugged the door closed behind her before stepping next to the wooden railing of the porch. "Fine. Maybe there are situations when fighting is the right thing to do. But the situations that call for it are a lot more serious than a little bully egging on my brother. I said I'll handle it and I will, even if I have to deal with Calvin's parents to do it."

"Don't go anywhere near Calvin's parents."

Something rippled down her spine. She'd never been particularly good at having someone tell her what she could and couldn't do.

She'd had the same reaction the first time someone had told her she was too young to take on raising Dillon. But her grandfather had believed she could, and that was what had mattered. She closed her hands over the rail. "There's no law I'd be breaking, Deputy. I'm perfectly free to have a civil discussion about their son and Dillon. For heaven's sake. They're little boys!"

"Abby." He covered her hands with his. Neither of them wore gloves, but his palms felt like hot irons in comparison to her cold fingers. "There's not much that ever stays civil where Bobby Pierce is concerned. I have a lot of experience with that family, and I'm *asking* you, for your sake, to keep your distance." He squeezed her hands.

Maybe if he wouldn't have done that—pressed his fingers so warmly, so familiarly against hers—she would have just taken his words for the advice they were. But he did, and she leaned forward until her face was barely a foot from his. She searched his eyes, wishing she knew what was going on inside. Wishing she knew if her attraction to him was so great that she'd only imagined he might feel the same. "I don't know what to make of you," she said huskily. "Is this just the deputy speaking, Sloan? Or is it someone else?"

"It's just me," he said evenly. "I wouldn't want to see anything happen to you or Dillon."

It was an answer, but a singularly frustrating one because she knew nothing more than she ever had. Which was a big fat zilch.

"For whatever reason, Dillon has taken to you," she said finally. "He's telling you things he won't tell me. And while I appreciate that, *I* don't want him hurt. Not by Calvin Pierce." She moistened her dry lips. "And…and not by you." Sloan had already told her he was with the sheriff's office for only a few more months. He'd never said what he intended to do after that. She wasn't so wet behind the ears as to think he'd be around for Dillon forever.

His gaze turned even more inward. "You're a smart woman, Abby. Dillon's lucky to have you."

And that was it.

That was all he said.

Because he turned and walked back across the yard, got into his SUV and drove away.

Chapter Seven

"Remind me when we play again not to bet against you," Dee said the next night as they carried the folding chairs she'd brought to Abby's back out to her car and stacked them in the trunk. There'd been eight of them playing, and though the competition was fierce, there had been just as much gossiping, pizza eating and margarita drinking going on as there had been shuffling cards. "You're a shark in sheep's clothing. Who taught you how to play poker?"

Abby set the last chair in Dee's trunk and stepped back so the other woman could shut it. "My grandfather. He also taught me how to shoot and how not to spit into the wind."

Dee was wearing her usual mischievous grin. "The man did too good of a job. I can't afford to lose like that. Don't earn enough teaching." She looked past Abby toward Sloan's darkened house. "Was hoping to catch a glimpse of Deputy Hottie."

Abby didn't have to look over her shoulder to know

that Sloan wasn't there. His SUV hadn't returned since he had given them a ride home from school the day before. "And here I thought you were the last to leave because you wanted to help me clean up the mess." She hadn't pulled on a coat before bringing out the chairs, and the night air was cold through her long-sleeve turtleneck. "Why do you care so much about Deputy McCray, anyway, when Principal *Gage* is the one you want?"

Dee peered at her. "Who told you that?"

"Nobody had to tell me. I have eyes."

The other woman's lips twisted. "Wish Joe Gage had eyes."

"Ask him out." She knew the principal wasn't married or otherwise involved. "Open his eyes for him."

"Easier said than done. He's the boss. Dating one of his employees is against the rules."

"Some rules are meant to be broken." Only as soon as she said the words, they reminded her of Sloan telling her that it wasn't always wrong to fight, and even though she'd vowed not to, she glanced back at his house.

"The school board also has some pretty strict rules," Dee was saying. "And I need my job. So…" She trailed off and lifted her shoulders. "I can't have his body, but I can have the pleasure of watching the man's backside whenever he's walking down the hallway at school. It's a poor substitute," she lamented with a wicked smile, "but it's all I've got."

Abby couldn't help but laugh. "You're terrible."

"I am. Everyone in town will tell you so." Dee gave her a quick hug and then pulled open her car door. "Sorry if we were too noisy for Dillon once he went to bed."

"It was fine." She'd checked on her brother a few times throughout the evening. He'd fallen asleep reading a book. She hoped he managed to make it till morning without a bad dream. He'd awakened twice with nightmares the night before. So even though she'd been horrified about his school suspension, it was just as well, because they'd both fallen asleep for a few hours in the middle of the afternoon as a result of their disturbed night. "And I had a lot of fun. So thanks again for inviting yourselves to my place."

Dee chuckled. "Anytime." Then she got inside her car and drove away.

Abby rubbed her hands up and down her arms. The sky was clear again, black and studded with stars. Only two of the houses on the street had lights on inside at this late an hour: hers and Mr. Gilcrest's next door. She'd met the elderly man the week before when she'd taken over a plate of chocolate cookies. It had been the neighborly thing to do. Just as it had been the neighborly thing to do to bake cookies for Sloan. It meant exactly the same thing.

On the surface, it worked. Underneath, though, she knew that was plain malarkey.

She sighed and turned around, her boots crunching through the snow as she headed back across the yard. The scarf around Frosty's neck was looking decidedly bedraggled, and his cookie eyes and carrot nose had disappeared days ago. She stopped in front of him and his smaller companion, who was scarfless and faceless because Abby had interrupted Dillon and Sloan while they'd been making him.

"Well, guys. I'd invite you inside for hot chocolate, but I don't think you'd survive it."

"They say the first sign is when you start talking to snowmen."

She nearly jumped out of her skin, yelping as she whirled to see Sloan standing in the middle of the street. "*Must* you do that?"

"Do what?"

"Sneak up and startle the life out of me!"

He came closer, and she realized his dark clothing wasn't his uniform at all, but running clothes. He looked more like a wide receiver geared up for a workout than an off-duty deputy. "Sorry."

"No, you're not," she countered. "You're like little boys everywhere who enjoy sneaking up on little girls just to see them jump." He was so far from boyish that it was ridiculous, but the assessment made her feel better. "Do you always go out running in the middle of the night? Where's your truck?"

"Sometimes. And it's at the office." He came a little closer. His head was bare. "I don't always bring it home, and I'm off duty until Monday morning. I've got my own wheels, too."

She'd been living there nearly two weeks and had seen him drive nothing other than that sheriff's SUV. "Where are you hiding them? In your attic?"

His teeth flashed. Just for a moment.

Or maybe that was her wishful thinking.

She'd told him to go away, and he had. It was still the smart thing to do, so she had no business having wishful thoughts where he was concerned.

"In my garage."

"Are you talking about that dinky shed behind your house?" If he was, his car would have to be even smaller than her little sedan. It was hard to picture.

"None other." He stepped over the chunks of grit-filled snow at the edge of the street. "It's nearly midnight. Little girls shouldn't be out so late."

She'd been the one to use the term first, but when *little girl* came from him, it reminded her how young he really considered her. "Maybe I had a date," she said blithely.

"A threesome with Frosty and his snow-bro?" He came closer. "I'm thinking probably...no date."

She shivered. Lifted her chin. "You don't know everything."

"I know you wouldn't leave Dillon."

Caught, darn it all. Her chin lowered. "I had some friends over."

"Girlfriends."

Her breath escaped on a puff. *"Friends."* She was completely out of her depth with him. Didn't even really know what they were doing talking in the middle of the night on her front lawn.

"*Girl*friends," he pushed again.

She pressed her lips together. Shivered some more and crossed her arms tightly. It was mid-January, and the temperature was hovering below freezing.

So why did she feel so hot inside?

"Why does it matter to you if they were *girls*—" she drew out the word the way Dillon would "—or not?"

"It shouldn't." He took another step. Stopped within arm's reach of her. "But it does."

Her spurt of bravery disappeared. Her heart thumped hard inside her chest, as if she'd been the one out having a midnight run.

"I don't like thinking of you with another man."

She dug her fingertips into her arms. Her nails poked hard. She wasn't dreaming. "Dee Crowder from school," she said faintly. "And some friends of hers. We...we played poker. I won."

Again, a brief flash of white teeth. "That's my girl."

"I'm not your girl." She shifted her feet, and the snow creaked under her boots.

"Half the town keeps telling me that you are."

She swallowed. Moistened her lips. The heat inside her

was rising up her neck, and she wanted to claw at the snug turtleneck that felt as if it was strangling her. "I'm not your girl," she whispered.

He took another step. It was either stand her ground or back up into the snowmen. Sloan didn't touch her, but she still felt the heat radiating off him as he lowered his head until his mouth brushed against her ear. "If you were—" his deep voice was soft "—we wouldn't be standing out here freezing." His gloved hand slid against her neck. Curved beneath her jaw. Her knees felt like melting wax. "I'd have you in bed...." His lips grazed her earlobe.

She moaned a little, knowing she ought to protest, even if she suspected he was right. "Sloan—" She twisted her head until her mouth found his.

And then it didn't matter that he'd been avoiding her for days. It didn't matter that they were standing alone in the middle of the night in the middle of her front yard. And it didn't matter whose girl she was or was not.

There was only the taste of his mouth. His tongue. The ridge of his teeth. There was only the feel of his chest, warm and hard against her as she wrapped her arms around him.

When he tore his mouth away, far too soon, she made a protesting sound. "Don't stop." She kissed his jaw. Tried to reach his lips again. "Sloan—"

He caught the back of her head and tucked it against his chest. His mouth brushed her ear again. "We have to stop. Or I'm not going to be able to."

"Would that be so bad?"

His chest moved with the groan he let out. "I'm pretty sure it wouldn't be *bad*." He kissed the top of her head, and his voice turned serious. "You were right to want to protect Dillon. And you should want to protect yourself. You don't need a man like me in your life."

She turned her head. Listened to the fast beat of his heart. "Why not?"

"Too many reasons to count." He ran his hands down her spine. "I'm not a good man, Abby."

"You're a hero."

He went still.

"I recognized your name when you first told me," she admitted softly. "Braden isn't cut off from the rest of the world. I know what you did. How you brought down the Deuce's Cross and that guy, Johnny…whatever his name was."

"Diablo." His chest moved with the deep sigh he let out. "Not everything about that situation made it into the newspapers. I might have done my job, but it was everyone around me who had to pay the price for it. Believe me, sweetheart. That is not what heroes do. I hurt too many people, and I don't want you to be another. If I were a better man, I'd have never touched you."

She couldn't feel the cold from the outside anymore. This time it was slowly seeping from the inside. "Then why did you?"

But he didn't answer. "First time I saw you, I thought Dillon was your son," he said instead.

She let out a short laugh even though she felt more like crying. And that wasn't something she was going to do because it would just be one more thing he'd feel responsible for causing. "That would be a challenge since I—" She realized what she was about to admit and broke off. "Nope. Not my son."

"But you're the only mom he's got, whether you carry the title or not."

She exhaled. "The only one who really believed I could do it was my grandfather."

"I believe you can do it."

Which just sealed the deal on tears stinging her eyes, no matter how much she wanted to keep them at bay.

I could love this man. The realization filled her head. *If only he'd let me.*

His hands slid to her shoulders, steadying her, even as he took a step back. A step away.

"It's late. You should go inside. Go to bed."

Where she'd lie, alone, and wish for him. A man she knew so little about. "What about you?"

"I'll keep running."

"Until you can sleep?"

His lips twisted. "Sure."

Something about the way he hesitated caught at her. "Do you have nightmares, Sloan?" He just looked at her and cocked his head slightly. "Dillon does. That morning that you were there wasn't the first, but at least they're coming less often. When he wakes from them he runs to me."

"He's a smart kid." He jerked his chin toward the house. "Go inside, Abby."

That was the smartest course. It was cold. It was late.

Sloan didn't want things to go further with her, and she ought to be grateful that he had the self-control that she didn't.

Everyone *she'd* ever loved had left her, too. Her mother hadn't wanted her. Her grandfather had died. Her grandmother had forgotten. Dillon, too, one day would grow up and go out to live his own life, and that was how it should be.

"Don't run too far," she said softly. And then, before she lost what little sense she had and begged him to come with her no matter what the consequences, she circled around Frosty and his friend and went inside.

She closed the door quietly and leaned back against it, closing her eyes.

There was no sound of Sloan following her up the steps. He wasn't standing on the other side of the door, prepared to knock softly and tell her that he'd changed his mind.

There was nothing but silence.

She moved away from the door and turned off the lights, one by one. When the house was dark, she went to the front window.

Sloan stood in the middle of the street. Tall. Broad shouldered. But still little more than a shadow in the moonlight.

She'd never really wondered before what loneliness looked like. But now she knew it looked like him.

And even though she knew he couldn't see her through the window, it was as if he did, because he turned then and disappeared into the night.

She wiped her wet cheeks and went to bed.

The sun was streaming across his bed when Sloan waked the next day. He rolled onto his back, throwing his arm over his eyes. Since he hadn't gone to sleep until well after the sun had come up in the first place, the presence of sunlight didn't say a helluva lot about what time it was.

The television was still on, reruns of headline news droning in the background. He could hear the sound of high-pitched laughter coming from outside, though, so he shoved aside the blankets and walked naked through his second floor until he could look out the window overlooking the front of the house. He didn't worry about being seen. The window was too high.

But it was just right for looking out.

Dillon was running around both his yard and Sloan's with the mangiest-looking dog he'd ever seen, and he wondered where it had come from. The fact that Abby was there, too, her shining brown hair bouncing around the shoulders of her bright red coat, told him there was no cause for worry.

And seeing the smiles on both of the Marcums' faces made it all worth watching.

So he did, until his phone started ringing and he had to go and answer it.

He was off duty for the next two days, but that didn't mean he couldn't get called in if the necessity arose. He grabbed the extension in his bedroom. "McCray."

"Clay," his sister responded with a laugh. "Nice way to answer the phone, Bean."

He raked his hand down his bristly cheeks and tucked the phone against his shoulder while he pulled on his jeans. "What's wrong?"

"Nothing!" She sighed noisily. "You're too quick to think the worst. I'm just calling to let you know that Sunday dinner is here at our place tomorrow. We're having pizza from Pizolli's. *Please* consider coming."

Sunday dinner to the Clays—which now included his sister—meant a weekly family dinner where they all got together as though it was a damn holiday or something. In the months that he'd been in Weaver, he'd succeeded in missing most of them.

"I know you're not on duty," she went on. "Because I had Sarah ask Max."

He grimaced. "Your being cousins-in-law with my boss's wife has a real downside."

"Bring your friend Abby and her brother along," she went on as if he'd never spoken.

"We're just neighbors." The lie was blatant. He didn't much care.

Neither did his sister, evidently, because she ignored him. "Mallory's on duty at the hospital, but Ryan came into the shop this morning to buy Chloe a new dress, and he said they'd all be there. I know that Chloe and Dillon are in the same class at school. She'll have someone to play with if you bring Abby and her little brother."

God help him. There were just too many freaking members of this family that his sister had married into. Ryan was yet another one of Axel's cousins. "And if you can't succeed with me, you'll make me feel guilty because of Ryan's little girl."

"Whatever works," she said blithely. "We're just having pizza. I'll expect you around three."

As if it were a done deal, she hung up.

He listened to the dial tone for a moment. Then he stared at the receiver before replacing it on the cradle and shaking his head.

Marriage and motherhood had made Tara downright sassy.

He pinched the bridge of his nose, willing away the pain that was there courtesy of too little sleep, and went into the bathroom.

The mirror showed what it always did. The same gray in his dark hair that his dad had also had at Sloan's age. The same lines radiating from his bloodshot eyes that he'd earned riding with Johnny Diablo and the Deuces. The same tattoo he'd gotten the first year he'd rode with them. The scar from the gunshot courtesy of Maria's crazy-assed brother two years ago was still on his biceps, a long, narrow trench of white, puckered tissue.

He looked the way he always did.

Like hell.

He heard the laughter from outside again, sounding closer, so he headed to the bedroom again and peered through the blinds to see a streak of red dart through the snow between his house and Abby's.

He went back into the bathroom and flipped on the

shower. The rush of water at least drowned out the sounds from outside. It didn't do a thing, though, to drown out the memory of kissing her. And it didn't do a thing to stop his imagination from conjuring more, not even when he turned the water stone cold and it felt as if he were being pelted with bits of ice.

Sexual frustration was easy enough to cure. All he'd have to do was find a woman who wanted nothing but sex. Easy enough to accomplish. He'd done it before.

But she wouldn't be Abby.

Feeling about as cheerful as a junkyard dog, he pulled on warm clothes, grabbed his helmet out of the hall closet and stomped out the back door of his house.

God had some mercy on him, because the only sign of Abby behind his house were her footprints in the snow.

He rolled his bike out of the garage—which really was nothing more than a glorified shed—and swung his leg over the seat, kicking the engine to life. Despite the fact that he rode the thing only a few times a month these days, the engine roared and he felt an almost guilty pleasure from the sound.

He rode over the snow-covered alley behind the houses to the end of the short block and turned out onto the street.

And then he just rode.

Chapter Eight

Abby watched the black monster of a bike disappear around the corner while she tried to clip the leash onto Rex's collar.

Sloan's wheels, she realized.

The scary-looking bike suited a man who went running in the middle of the night in the dead of winter.

"Was that Sloan? I didn't know he had a motorcycle." She hadn't thought it possible, but Dillon sounded even more reverent about their neighbor.

"I didn't know, either." She turned her attention to the leash. The overexcited dog wasn't having any part of it; he wriggled out of her grip and bounded over to Dillon again, jumping against him with such enthusiasm that he lost his balance and landed on his butt in the snow.

Her brother's laughter filled the air as he rolled around on the ground with the dog. It had been an impetuous decision to bring the dog home from Shop-World, where a rescue organization had set up camp for the day. She simply hadn't been able to resist. Dillon had been so taken with the two-year-old mutt, whose wiry coat had too many colors to count or define. He'd fallen in love with Rex on the spot. And maybe it was only because she needed something else to love, but Abby had, too.

So despite the fact that she was trying to impress on Dillon the importance of not fighting at school, back into the big store they'd gone, where they'd purchased dog food and a leash and a dog bed that Abby hoped she'd be able to get Rex to use instead of Dillon's bed.

She caught up to the dog and finally managed to click on the leash. He immediately managed to tangle it around her legs, nearly taking her to the ground as effectively as he had Dillon. She succeeded in unwinding herself and handed the end of the leash to Dillon. The swelling on his face had gone down, only to be replaced by a bluish bruise in the corner of his eye. "Let's see how he does walking to the park."

They got to the park fine, though Abby wasn't sure if Dillon was walking Rex or if it were the other way around. Then she held the leash while Dillon played on the swings for a while. They creaked loudly in the cold, but they worked, nevertheless.

She sat on the bench nearby, enjoying the welcome warmth of the sun. All in all, it should have been a perfect day, and it would have been if she didn't have such an ache inside her.

"Pretty hard to get a decent suntan when we're covered up to our ears with coats and scarves, isn't it?"

Abby smiled with delight as she recognized the woman who plopped on the bench beside her. "Hayley! What are you doing here?"

"Trying to get in a little exercise," Hayley Templeton

said ruefully. "A friend of mine is supposed to meet me here." She stretched out her legs and wiggled her running shoes. "I heard through the grapevine that you'd moved here from Braden. How's everything going?"

That particular grapevine, Abby knew, would be in the form of her talkative high-school mate Delia, who was Hayley's cousin. "It's new," she said, glancing at Dillon. He'd taken to jumping out of the swing when it was at its height, and Rex barked every time. "We're settling in. I haven't talked to Delia in a while. I didn't know you were here in Weaver."

As quickly as she'd sat, Hayley rose and propped her foot on the bench, stretching. "A little over a year ago I took over a practice here from a psychologist who was retiring. I do mostly family counseling right now." She switched legs. "I was sorry to hear about your grandfather. He was a good teacher. I wouldn't have made it through any of my math classes in high school if it hadn't been for him. And now, even as a nurse, you're working at a school, too."

Abby smiled ruefully. "I am."

"What about your grandmother? How's she doing?"

"She's at Braden Bridge full-time now."

The psychologist straightened. Her eyes were kind. "Alzheimer's is such a cruel disease. How are *you* doing?" She looked over at the little boy playing on the swings. "And your brother? It's Dillon, right?"

Abby nodded. "We're managing." Aside from her being dangerously close to falling for her neighbor, and Dillon's fight at school, everything was just dandy.

"Well." Hayley pulled her foot down from the bench. "If you ever need to talk, just let me know." She waved at the other jogger who'd just entered the park before leaning over to pet Rex on the head, much to his delight. "You're a cutie."

Abby laughed at that. The dog was homely in the extreme with a head that didn't fit his body and a body that didn't fit his short little legs. "We adopted him this morning from a rescue."

The other jogger reached them. "Do you know Sam Dawson?" Hayley asked.

Abby shook the other woman's hand, recognizing her from the school assembly. "You're with the sheriff's department."

Sam smiled. "Guilty as charged." She was jogging in place, and she gave Hayley a wry look. "You're already thinking about wimping out for a cinnamon roll over at Ruby's, aren't you?"

"Maybe," Hayley allowed. She grinned at Abby. "The disadvantage of having Sam as a running partner is that she never wimps out."

"Would lose my job pretty quickly if I did," Sam said dryly. "Nice meeting you, Abby," she said as she started off along the path.

"Exercising is such a *chore,*" Hayley admitted. But she dutifully set off after the other woman.

Dillon jumped off his swing again and trotted over to kneel next to Rex. "Can *we* go to Ruby's and have a cinnamon roll?"

She might have known that he'd overhear that. But since it was lunchtime and she didn't have any real desire for peanut butter and jelly sandwiches at home, she agreed. "You have to have some real lunch, though, too."

"Can we take Rex?"

"We'll tie him up outside the diner." She pushed to her feet and handed Dillon the leash again. "Rex needs to mind you," she said. "Not the other way around."

Fine words. Rex dragged Dillon—and then Abby, too, when she took over the leash—all the way to the diner. She latched the leash around the light post that was outside the diner door, and they went inside. It was already crowded, the booths and tables filled, but there were several stools at the counter that were free, so they sat there.

Dillon got a kick out of that. He liked seeing everything that went on behind the counter. He took forever reading through all the specials that were written on a board before he decided on a grilled cheese sandwich.

As soon as the girl took their order, Dillon twirled on the padded red seat and faced the crowded diner behind them. He kicked one leg absently. "If Deputy McCray's not your boyfriend, how come you was kissing him last night?"

It was as if every person in the restaurant went silent, just so they could hear Dillon's high, boyish voice.

Abby's face was on fire. She gave Dillon a stern look, even though it wasn't *his* fault that he'd seen what she'd been doing the night before. "Turn around and eat your lunch."

He looked over his shoulder at his place mat. "I don't got any lunch."

"You don't *have* any lunch," she corrected. "Turn around and drink your milk, then."

He sighed noisily and turned around. "Why are you mad?"

"I'm not mad."

"Then why do you got a—*have*—a frowny face?"

Abby stifled a groan and mentally smoothed out her expression. "I'm not frowning. And what were you doing up in the middle of the night last night, anyway?" She'd looked in on him the way she always did, and he'd been sound asleep. "Did you have a bad dream?"

"Nah. I was thirsty."

"Gotta love kids," a voice said beside her. Abby looked over to the petite brunette who was standing at the counter paying her bill. "They say the darndest things, don't they?" The woman stuck out her hand. "Tara Clay," she introduced herself. "And you're Abby."

Abby managed a weak smile and shook her hand. "Yes. Abby Marcum. Nice to meet you."

Tara had eyes as dark as chocolate, which crinkled slightly at the corners as her smile widened even more. "I'm Sloan's sister," she said meaningfully.

"Oh!" Abby's stomach dropped. "I…suppose you heard my brother."

Tara laughed softly. "Honey, everyone in here heard your brother. Don't look so upset, though. We've all survived people in this town talking about us." She looked past Abby to Dillon. "Your dog's doing a good job greeting everyone who comes in here. What's his name?"

Dillon stared shyly at Sloan's sister. "Rex," he whispered.

Abby sorely wished he'd have whispered earlier.

"Good name." Tara tucked her change into her purse as the waitress settled Abby's and Dillon's lunches on the counter. "I told Sloan earlier that he should bring you two along for dinner tomorrow," she said after the waitress had gone again.

"Oh, but—"

"We're getting together for pizza. Nothing fancy. Pizolli's. They're new but good."

"Pizolli's *is* good, but—"

"That's settled, then." Tara smiled brightly. "I'd stay to chat longer, but I've got to get back to the shop." And just like that, she hurried out the door.

"Sloan's sister looks like Snow White," Dillon commented, catching a melting string of cheese from his sandwich with the tip of his tongue.

Her shoulders sagged. "I guess she does." Dillon didn't know how embarrassing his question had been. But she didn't want a repeat of it, either. Not in the crowded diner. So she hurried him through his lunch and had his cinnamon roll wrapped to take with them. When he started to protest, she reminded him of poor Rex, tied up and waiting outside in the cold.

He needed no further prompting and barely waited long enough for her to pay the check before going outside. He stopped short, though, at the sight of the woman and boy crossing the street toward them.

Abby recognized Calvin and assumed that the thin, tense-looking woman with him was his mother.

There was no point in pretending they hadn't all seen one another. Not right there on the sidewalk outside of Ruby's.

She put her hand on Dillon's shoulder. Even through the puffy coat, she could feel the way he'd gone tense. Rex, leash twisted around the light post, thumped his tail, whining excitedly as he waited for Dillon's attention. "Untangle Rex," she suggested softly.

Calvin—with a bruise on his eye nearly identical to Dillon's—was glaring at her brother, and Calvin's mother looked as if she wanted to be anywhere other than where they were.

When faced with an uncomfortable situation, Abby's grandmother had always suggested heading straight on into it. Better to meet it with some control, Minerva used to say.

And this was a distinctly uncomfortable situation.

Abby stuck out her gloved hand, walking toward Calvin's mother. "Mrs. Pierce," she greeted calmly. "I'm Abby Marcum. Dillon's sister. It's nice to meet you."

The other woman looked a little confused. A little fearful. As if she didn't quite know what to do about Abby's extended hand. But after a brief hesitation, she extended her own hand, awkwardly shaking the tips of Abby's fingers before quickly pulling back. "You, too," she said half under her breath.

"I'm sorry about the trouble between the boys at school," Abby forged on despite the wholesale lack of encouragement coming from Calvin's mother. "I just want to assure you that nothing like that will happen again." She looked at her brother. "Will it, Dillon," she prompted.

He was crouched down hugging Rex as though the dog was his last friend in the world. His gaze flicked to Calvin. Then his face turned mutinous. "Will if he calls me a liar again."

"Dillon!"

He didn't look at her; he just ducked his head against Rex.

Her grandmother hadn't given her any words of wisdom to prepare for situations like *this,* and Abby wished she'd have just followed Sloan's advice to keep her distance from the Pierce family.

She gave Calvin's mother an apologetic look. "I'm sorry. I don't know what's gotten into—"

"Figures you'd have the ugliest dog in the world," Calvin sneered, interrupting.

"Hush your mouth." His mother swatted his shoulder. "Don't mind him," she told Abby. "He's wanted a dog forever."

"If I *did* have a dog, it wouldn't be no dinky excuse like that."

"Rex *isn't* dinky," Dillon defended, hopping to his feet. Rex, still tied to the post, bared his teeth and growled.

"Rex, be quiet." Abby casually sidestepped so she was

standing between the dog and the Pierces. "There's a res-cue group with all sorts of dogs out at Shop-World today," she shared. "The only fee we had to pay for Rex was for the dog license. Which was a good thing, because that's about all I could afford," she added lightly, just in case Mrs. Pierce took offense.

"Calvin's daddy doesn't much care for dogs."

Abby managed not to wince. She felt as if she were dig-ging herself in deeper. Despite her effort to be a barrier between Rex and Calvin, the little boy was still manag-ing to antagonize the young dog, kicking bits of gravel-ridden snow toward him. "Well." She smiled warmly. "I didn't mean to keep you out here in the cold." Calvin's mother's coat looked threadbare, and while Dillon's coat was too big for him, Calvin's was definitely too small. "I just wanted to say how sorry I was for everything." She reached down and unfastened the leash from the light post and kept a tight grip on it when Rex took a little lunge, growling again.

She couldn't really blame the dog when Calvin was deliberately taunting him. She took Dillon's hand. "Hope you enjoy the rest of your weekend," she told Mrs. Pierce as she tugged boy and dog with her away from the diner.

She waited until they were well out of earshot before she looked down at Dillon. "What were you thinking, tell-ing Calvin that you'd fight him again?"

Dillon didn't answer. He was focused on something else. Some*one* else, she realized quickly when Sloan stepped into their path.

"What were you thinking, talking to Lorraine Pierce in the first place," he asked.

She felt frazzled. First his sister in Ruby's, then the Pierces. And now him? "What are you doing here?"

He glanced over his shoulder at the building next to

him, and she realized she'd walked Dillon right past the sheriff's office. "Lying in wait for you," he said blandly.

Her lips tightened. "We ran into Calvin and his mother outside of Ruby's. I wasn't going to be rude and just ignore her. We ran into your sister inside Ruby's, too," she added before he could get on his soapbox about the Pierces.

His eyes narrowed. "Tara."

"Do you have another sister?" Her spurt of smart-i-tude fizzled. "Yes. Tara. She's very nice."

"She is," he agreed.

She'd considered warning him about Dillon being overheard inside the diner. But heading straight on to that particular awkwardness was a lot more difficult than facing Calvin and his mother.

So she focused on the least explosive thing she could. "She must be the official welcoming committee for Weaver. She invited us out for pizza tomorrow afternoon."

He didn't show any sort of reaction, but Abby still sensed his sudden unease.

"We can't," she added as if she hadn't noticed his reaction. A girl had her pride, after all. "We're going to Braden to visit my grandmother."

That got Dillon's attention in a hurry. "We are?"

She squeezed his hand, hoping he'd get the message.

"Not that your sister gave me a chance to tell her that."

"Sounds like Tara."

She moistened her lips, searching her mind vainly for some safe topic. But it turned out she didn't need one because Sloan's brown eyes mercifully focused on Dillon as he hunkered down to pet Rex. While her brother chattered on about how they'd adopted him that morning, Abby surreptitiously studied Sloan.

She knew his hair was thick and felt as slippery as satin

Send For
2 FREE BOOKS
Today!

I accept your offer!

Please send me two free
Harlequin® Special Edition
novels and two mystery gifts
(gifts worth about $10).
I understand that these books
are completely free—even
the shipping and handling will
be paid—and I am under no
obligation to purchase anything, ever,
as explained on the back of this card.

235/335 HDL F44T

Please Print

FIRST NAME

LAST NAME

ADDRESS

APT.# | CITY

STATE/PROV. | ZIP/POSTAL CODE

Visit us online at
www.ReaderService.com

through her fingers. Knew the shadow on his jaw felt sexily abrasive against her palms.

What she didn't know was what made him tick. What he believed and cared about.

What caused his restlessness.

Even though she knew it was better to remain uninvolved, she couldn't help wanting to understand him. It was a desire that came dangerously close to need.

Which would get her nowhere. Inexperienced or not, she wasn't a fool. She wasn't looking to get hurt. Even though she couldn't imagine ever forgetting how it had felt to be in his arms.

"You could come, you know," he said abruptly. "After you visit your grandmother."

All her sensible thoughts screeched to a halt, and she stared at him.

"Tomorrow afternoon," he added, as if she needed clarification. "Unless you were planning to spend the entire day in Braden. Dillon would have a few kids to chase around with, too."

Dillon tugged at her arm. "Can we? I wanna chase around."

She let out half a laugh that sounded as helpless as she felt. Just when she started to think she had a course set, had her path laid out clearly before her where I'm-No-Hero Sloan was concerned, he tossed a wrench in the works.

"I do like Pizolli's," she finally said. It was a small family restaurant, and Sloan was right: there were usually a few kids for Dillon to play with. "Your, uh, your sister told me that's what the plan was. I suppose we could be back from Braden in time." Plenty of time. It would take only a few hours coming and going. And Minerva didn't tolerate visitors well for any length of time. It distressed her when she knew she ought to recognize them but didn't.

"Good." Sloan straightened and his eyes roved over her, which had the usual result of making her knees feel wobbly. "It's settled, then."

The comment was exactly like his sister's. As if whatever concerns or questions Abby might still have were moot.

"Will you give me a ride on your motorcycle?"

Abby closed her hand over Dillon's shoulder. "Honey, you can't just ask people things like that."

Sloan's lips twitched. "It's okay." He lifted the helmet he was holding. "You can wear this. It'll be too big for you, but we're not going much farther than around the corner to your house. Long as Abby says it's okay."

Dillon looked as if Christmas had just come all over again. He looked up at Abby. *"Puhleeze?"*

She pointed her finger toward Sloan. "Straight back to the house."

He lifted his palm. "Swear it."

She was such a sucker, swayed by the amusement lighting his expression. "You'll have to mind him for a few minutes until I catch up with you."

He looked even more amused. "Think we can manage not to burn down anything. Take your time."

Dillon eagerly handed her Rex's leash and latched his hand around Sloan's as if he were afraid the man might change his mind.

Abby caught the flicker of emotion on Sloan's face and ached inside. It seemed so obvious to her that he was a man who cared. Who *wanted* to care. So why wouldn't he let himself?

She stifled a sigh and eyed her brother. "Hold on and do everything that Sloan tells you to do."

Dillon nodded so hard the hood on his coat bounced.

"It's just a motorcycle ride," Sloan murmured. "We're not going skydiving."

She made a face. "Might as well be."

"Never been on a bike?"

"Sure. The two-wheeled kind that depends on pedaling for power." Feeling oddly bereft now that Dillon was holding Sloan's hand and not hers, she scooped Rex off his feet and cuddled him against her chest. The dog trembled with delight and tried to lick her face. She lifted her chin out of range, and he transferred his adoration to her wrist.

"Deputy McCray would give you a ride, too," Dillon said. "Wouldn'tcha?" His young voice was filled with utter faith.

She focused on Rex, rubbing his head. It was safer than looking at Sloan, since she was afraid her face probably showed the same bare emotion as her seven-year-old brother's. "I don't have any desire to ride on the back of that thing, so it doesn't matter anyway."

"Think your sister's afraid," Sloan told Dillon, sounding very man to man.

"You don't have to be afraid, Abby," Dillon assured her earnestly. "You won't fall or nothing."

"Or anything," she corrected faintly. But she was afraid. Not of falling off but of falling, period.

And a few minutes later, as she watched Sloan ride slowly down the street on his big black monster with Dillon attached to his back like a little limpet, she was afraid it might already be too late.

Chapter Nine

Sloan was still kicking himself the next afternoon as he checked out his usual cruiser and drove over to pick up Abby and Dillon.

He could have left things as they were. Abby and Dillon would have spent the day in Braden visiting their grandmother, just as she'd planned. No harm. No foul.

He'd told her he needed to keep his distance.

How was asking her to his sister's—for their weekly family dinner, for God's sake—keeping his distance?

He'd thought that taking the bike out would clear his head. And it had. It had cleared his head of every bit of sense he'd ever possessed.

The second he pulled into Abby's driveway, her front door flew open and Dillon raced out. Abby, coatless, followed hard on his heels but only to catch Rex, who'd darted out, as well.

In a competition between Abby and the homely little

pup, she was outmatched. Whenever she zigged, the dog zagged, bounding over the snow as though he had springs in his short legs.

Sloan got out of the SUV to join the chase. It helped him stop thinking about his insanity, at least. He pointed at the corner of the yard. "Dillon, keep Rex from getting past you over there."

Dillon ran toward the area, snow kicking up under his heels. Then he turned, bracing his feet wide apart and crouching a little.

He looked like a miniature linebacker. A very thin, very short linebacker, maybe, but if the determination on Dillon's face was any indication, he was going to stop Rex, come hell or high water.

Sloan didn't know where the urge to laugh came from. It was just there. Same way his head went clear when he rode. He stifled the sound with a cough, though, and gestured for Abby to take the opposite corner, between the back of his SUV and the street. Sloan took a third corner, between her yard and his. Rex, caught in the middle, bounced toward Dillon, yipping with excitement at this latest game.

"Don't let him get past you," Abby called out. "He'll head for Sloan's backyard like he did yesterday." Her eyes were bright and shining as she looked at Sloan. "He climbed behind your woodpile, and I would've never gotten him out if he hadn't chosen to chase after Mr. Gilcrest's cat instead."

"That grumpy old man's got a cat? Since when?"

"He told me he's had Marigold for years. And what do you mean by *grumpy?* As long as you don't make the mistake of bringing up the federal government, he's perfectly friendly." She danced around a little when it seemed as if Rex was going to turn her way. But the wily dog tore around in a circle, heading off to the center of the yard, where he lifted his leg and did his business at the base of Deputy Frosty.

Sloan had lived in the neighborhood for half a year. He'd never seen Gilcrest's cat, much less heard of her.

Abby had been there less than a month and she found the old coot friendly.

He wanted to blame it on her youth—on naïveté. But he suspected it was simply *her*. Something about her that brought out the best in people.

"Oh, Dill—he's heading for you again!"

Dillon launched himself at the dog and landed face first. He got an armful of snow and not much else. Rex pounced on Dillon's back and ran up the slice of ground between their houses.

"Nuts," she muttered as she ran past Sloan, grabbed Dillon and set him on his feet and followed the dog toward the backyard. "Just call his name and see if he'll come back to you," she yelled.

Sloan walked over to Dillon and finished dusting the snow off his back. "You ever have a dog before?"

Dillon shook his head. "You?"

Sloan shook his head. "Nope."

"But you're old!"

Sloan winced. "Sometimes it seems that way," he allowed dryly.

Dillon's forehead crinkled. "How come?"

He figured the boy was still on the topic of dogs and not Sloan's state of decrepitude. "Because we never lived anywhere we could have one."

"How come?"

"Because we moved around a lot."

Dillon still looked curious. "How come?"

"You give *persistence* a new name, sport."

"Huh?"

He roughed up the boy's hair. It was as dark a brown as his sister's and just as soft. "Nothing. Run inside your house and get a handful of dog food or something."

"He's got treats!" Dillon darted over to the house and up the porch steps.

Rex wasn't going to go unloved, obviously. "A treat sounds good," he said, even though Dillon wasn't there to hear him.

The dog wouldn't be able to resist temptation.

He heard Abby's boots crunching on the snow as she returned. Her cheeks were as pink as the sweater she was wearing and her shiny hair was tousled.

It would look the same way if he ran his fingers through it.

Homely dogs weren't the only ones swayed by temptation.

Sloan had to shove his hands in his pockets to keep from reaching for her. "No luck getting the hound?"

"He went straight behind your woodpile again. I don't know what's back there that's so interesting to him. Where's Dillon?"

"There." He nodded toward the boy, who was racing out of the house waving a bone-shaped dog biscuit.

Abby made a face. "Silly I didn't think of that in the first place." They trooped to the rear of Sloan's house, and Dillon crouched next to the woodpile.

"That space doesn't look big enough for a rat to get through."

"Now there's a lovely thought." She grimaced. "You don't suppose there's something dead back there, do you?"

Sloan wished he would've kept his mouth shut. "Nah," he lied. How the hell would he know what kind of creatures dwelled or died behind the wood?

Dillon called the dog's name. "I've got a treat for you," he crooned. As if by magic, Rex gave a woof.

They all turned to see the dog standing behind them, his head cocked as if they were the ones doing something strange.

"Rex!" Dillon pounced on him, feeding him the biscuit at the same time. "Where'd you go, buddy? Huh?"

Abby looked from the woodpile to Rex and back again. "It's a mystery to me." Then she scooped up the wriggling dog herself. "I'll shut him in the house, and we can get going."

Sloan rubbed the dog's head. He had the face of a beagle, the body of a terrier and the short legs of a dachshund. Altogether it was quite a combination. "You could just bring him, you know."

"Tie him up outside Pizolli's?" Her brows pulled together. "I suppose so, but it's just as easy to leave him here. He's potty trained already—"

"Not at the restaurant. At Tara's."

Her lips parted and some of the rosiness seemed to drain out of her cheeks. "We're…going to your sister's house?"

"That's where they're getting together this week for Sunday dinner. Thought she told you."

Abby looked even more alarmed. "She invited us for pizza. Pizolli's. I assumed she meant at the restaurant."

Not with that crowd, he thought. They'd overrun the place. "Is there a problem?"

Her eyes were wide. "No," she said quickly. "I… We… just don't want to intrude." She moistened her lips, leaving them shiny and unintentionally inviting.

"Tara invited you," he reminded her. "Pretty sure she knew where she was inviting you *to*."

Her cheeks flushed again. "That's true, of course. But we can't show up with a dog in tow." Rex sighed heavily as if he felt disparaged. "It's bad enough I didn't offer to bring something." Panic had started to creep into her eyes again. "I don't have anything in the house to take. I should have dressed up nicer."

He couldn't help it. He grinned and slid his hand around her neck, tugging her close to kiss her forehead. "She's going to consider your presence gift enough. And believe me, sweetheart. There's not a damn thing wrong with the way you're dressed." She had on jeans that fit her perfect butt like a glove.

He let her go only to remember Dillon, who'd watched the brief exchange with his mouth open. "You *are* her boy-friend! You called her *sweetheart.*"

Abby looked pained. "Dillon, that doesn't mean any-thing."

The little boy ignored her, his eyes narrowing in on Sloan's face. "Grandpa used to call Grandma *sweetheart,*" he challenged. "And even though she doesn't 'member us, she still has a picture of him in her room."

"That's different." Abby handed him the dog. "Take Rex inside and make sure his water dish is full. You can give him another dog bone but be sure you close the front door before he gets out again. And bring my coat, please."

For a moment, Sloan wondered if the kid would argue. But he didn't. He just gave Sloan another close look then carried Rex back to the house.

Abby, on the other hand, looked anywhere other than at him. Her embarrassment was plain. "Sometimes he gets an idea that he just can't let go of." She laughed awkwardly. "A few months ago, he was convinced that there was a, uh…well, an alien…living in the attic. You know. Not-from-this-world sort of alien. Nothing I told him changed his mind."

He managed to keep a straight face. "Can't fault the kid for a lack of imagination. What finally worked?"

She lifted her shoulders. "Nothing. When the new owners moved into my grandparents' home, I had to keep Dillon away from them so he wouldn't let them know they weren't—" her voice dropped a register "—*alone.*"

"So you're saying I'm not going to be able to convince him I'm not your boyfriend."

Her cheeks turned even redder. "No! I'm just saying that— Oh, criminy." She all but stamped her foot in the snow. "I'll talk to him. That's what I'm saying. So don't worry about it."

The more uncomfortable she got, the more he relaxed. He was pretty sure that didn't say much about his character. "Do I look like I'm worried?"

Her gaze flew to him and skedaddled away just as quickly. Her soft lips compressed. She shook her head even as she lifted her shoulders.

A less decisive gesture didn't exist, and it made him want to scoop her close and kiss her crazy.

If you're going to be accused of being Abby's boyfriend anyway, why not take advantage of it?

He kicked the devil inside him to the corner.

"Didn't know all it took to be someone's boyfriend was to call her *sweetheart,*" he commented dryly, trying to steer things back on course. "Might have tried it a time or two when I was a kid."

Her cheeks were still red, but she gave a reluctant smile. "I'm sure you needed no help in that area."

"You'd be surprised." He closed his hands over her shoulders and steered her toward the driveway. "Pretty sure I've never qualified as anyone's boyfriend." There'd never been enough time when he'd been young. And then he'd gotten in with the ATF, and the stakes had turned too high. He'd loved Maria, and they'd been lovers. But not even during that relationship had anyone ever thought of him as her boyfriend. It would have been too normal.

Abby dug in her boots, and she gave him an incredulous look. "You're saying you've never been…you know, *with*—"

He realized where her mind had gone and nearly laughed. "I don't mean I haven't slept with a woman before."

"I know," she said defensively.

He brushed his finger down her nose. "Don't lie to a cop, sweetheart. We can always tell."

She exhaled noisily and marched to the driveway. "Why don't we take my car," she suggested. "I don't really want to ride behind the grille, where the doors don't open from the inside."

"I do," Dillon said, racing up to her and handing her the red coat. "I wanna ride in the back."

"Problem solved." Sloan reached past her to open the back door of the SUV, and Dillon climbed up inside.

Abby just looked stymied as she pulled on her coat. "I hope this isn't some indicator of the future," she muttered.

Sloan grinned and opened the passenger door for her. "I think you're safe. That boy's sense of right and wrong goes bone deep."

"Not deep enough to keep him from fighting with Calvin Pierce again. Threatening to, anyway." She didn't look at Sloan as she climbed inside, taking with her that fresh scent her hair always carried.

He rounded the vehicle and got behind the wheel. Old Gilcrest was sitting on his porch next door and actually had a benevolent-looking smile on his face. He held a fat orange cat in his arms and returned Abby's wave.

Sloan shook off his bemusement and backed out of the driveway.

After fastening her seat belt and making sure that Dillon had done the same, Abby sat facing forward, her arms crossed over her chest. "Where does your sister live?"

"Little ways out of town." It was an understatement. "First time I went out there, the road wasn't even paved. They've done some improvements since then." Nevertheless, the *cabin,* as they called the spacious house, was still off the beaten track.

"Do you catch a lot of bad guys back here?" Dillon sounded excited at the prospect.

He turned at the corner. "I've transported a few."

"Like on *Star Trek?*" Dillon giggled. "Beam me up, Scotty."

"Old television reruns," Abby offered, looking resigned.

"Captain Kirk and Mr. Spock were reruns when *I* was a kid. Didn't matter where we were living, I could always count on those old episodes." He smiled a little, thinking about it. "Tara and I would fight over channel control. She was more the *Brady Bunch* type."

Abby stirred. "He discovered *Star Trek* last year. Our grandmother was watching it one time when we visited, and he was hooked. Did you live in a lot of different places?"

"Thirty-some, I guess." He glanced at her and saw her shock.

"That explains the kindergarten classes," she said faintly. "The only place I've ever lived was in my grandparents' house in Braden. Well, other than here, obviously."

"Tara would have envied you. She hated all the moving around. Never having friends for more than a few months at a time. Never feeling settled."

Abby had relaxed her arms and turned slightly toward him. "But not you?"

He slowed automatically as they drove past the Pierce place. The sheet of plywood was still fixed over the broken picture window, but everything looked quiet; there was no indication at all that a troubled family was living inside. "I was always restless." He picked up his speed.

"And now?"

He could have given her a pat answer. Taken the easy way out. But he glanced at her, and the earnestness in her pretty eyes made it impossible. "It's something I'm trying to work out."

She pursed her soft lips in thought. "Is that why you haven't agreed to stay on permanently with the sheriff's department even though Max Scalise has asked?" She lifted her hands a little when he shot her a look. "Can't live in this town for more than a week without hearing someone mention it. It's not exactly a secret, is it?"

"A good reason *not* to live in this town," he muttered.

Her lashes swept down, and he turned his attention back to the road as Weaver became a reflection in his rearview mirror.

Dillon's voice popped up again. "I lived in Cheyenne."

Abby looked over her shoulder, obviously surprised at the admission. She caught Sloan's questioning look. "That's where he lived with his mother," she said under her breath.

Not our mother, but *his.* As if the woman hadn't had anything to do with Abby's existence at all. "And he usually doesn't talk much about living there," he concluded, just as quietly. "Reading your face is as easy as reading a book," he added.

"*That's* a comforting thought."

"And then I lived in Braden," Dillon continued blithely. "And now we live in Weaver."

"Where we'll be staying for a long time," Abby said firmly. "So if you're thinking you want to be like Sloan and live in another twenty-seven towns, you can just forget it. I *like* being settled in one place." She glanced at Sloan. "What did your parents do, anyway, that kept the wheels always rolling?"

"My dad was in the CIA."

Again, she looked shocked. "That sounds like something out of a movie."

"It wasn't anywhere near that interesting." He didn't want to get into their nightmarish childhood. He caught Dillon's gaze in the rearview mirror. "What's your favorite *Star Trek* episode?"

Beside him, Abby groaned a little.

"'The Trouble with Tribbles,'" Dillon said immediately. "We had a Tribble in our old house, you know. It lived in the attic."

Abby covered her face with her hands, and her shoulders shook slightly.

It took Sloan only a second to realize she was laughing, and soon he was, too.

It had been so long since he'd laughed—really laughed—that he laughed some more.

It seemed as though no time at all had passed when he turned off the highway onto a graded road full of curves and pulled up in front of his sister's place.

Abby stared at the half-dozen vehicles already parked in front of the big log house and felt alarm nudge its way into the pleasure she'd gained from hearing Sloan's deep laugh. "Looks like there are a lot of people here."

Humor still lurked in his dark eyes. "Astute detective work."

Rather than wait for Sloan to open her door for her—which seemed much too datelike—she pushed it open herself, leaving him to open Dillon's door instead. Then he led the way through the congestion of vehicles toward a wide porch.

There were two rocking chairs sitting on the porch, and judging by the blanket draped over the arm of one of them, they were actually being used even though it was the dead of winter. "My grandparents used to sit on their front porch in a glider. They were always holding hands."

"And Grandpa called her *sweetheart*," Dillon added, stomping up the stairs behind them.

She gave him a look. "Please don't start that again."

"It's the truth," he challenged.

"Yes, but—"

"You're here!" Tara had opened the front door and was smiling hugely over the head of the toddler she was carrying. "I was beginning to think big brave Deputy McCray had chickened out on me again." She waved them into the foyer, where she set the boy on his feet, only to redirect him when he tried to bolt out the front door. "Daddy will take you outside later, Aidan."

She was more successful at catching her son than Abby had been at catching Rex. The toddler went running back inside yelling for his daddy.

"It's my fault we ran late," Abby admitted.

"Our dog got out," Dillon added. He seemed to have forgotten his shyness with Sloan's sister as easily as he had with Sloan. "You look like Snow White."

Tara laughed, delighted. "And you look like Prince Charming," she returned, holding out her hand for him. "Let me show you our castle." She didn't glance back at them as she drew Dillon deeper into the house. "Show some manners, Bean, and take Abby's coat," she said.

Abby waited until Tara was out of earshot. "Bean?" She turned and tried not to shiver when his hands brushed her shoulders as he helped her out of her coat.

"Old nickname. Hers is worse."

Free of the coat, she turned to face him. He stood much closer than she'd expected, and she felt short of breath. "What is it?"

"Goober."

The glint in his eyes was so appealing it was all she could do to smother her laughter. "That *is* worse. But why Bean?"

"Nothing exciting. Mom used to harp on me to eat my beans." He grabbed her hand and pulled her in the same direction his sister had gone. Before she could make too much of it, he'd released her hand again as they entered a soaring great room dominated by enormous windows with a spectacular view of distant mountains. Vying for equal billing was a stone-fronted fireplace, where a welcoming fire crackled.

And in the middle of all of that were a dozen people sprawled around, plates of pizza on their laps. Abby felt herself flushing to the roots of her hair when their attention turned to her.

"Fortunately, we're a small group today," Tara said from across the room, where the pizza boxes were spread over a wide table. "So there's still some food left." She handed Dillon a plate, directing him to choose whatever he liked.

This was a small group? Abby hated to see what they'd consider a large one.

"Don't just stand there like a bump, Bean," Tara chided. "Introduce your girlfriend, already."

"We're just neighbors," Abby said, wishing the floor would open up and swallow her. "Friends."

Tara had a mischievous smile on her face, but she said nothing. She didn't have to.

"That isn't what I hear," a very slender blonde said from the corner of a chair where she was curled. "I'm Lucy, by the way. It's all over town how you two were getting all cozy on the front porch the other night." Her eyes danced merrily.

"And he calls her *sweetheart*," Dillon chimed in.

"Well, then," Tara concluded. "That seals the deal for me." She held up a plate in invitation. "Pizza?"

Chapter Ten

"So…" A few hours later, Tara stood next to Sloan at the kitchen sink, watching the rest of the family chase around outside in the snow with a football. "I like her."

No point pretending he didn't know whom she meant. Despite the trial by fire his sister and her family greeted them with, Abby managed to rise above it simply by wading right into the group, extending her hand to one person after another as she introduced herself. She didn't offer a single explanation about kisses or sweethearts or anything. Just was her usual friendly self as if the notion of being his girlfriend wasn't worth the breath of denying or confirming.

Now she was running around with the others, a grin as wide as Dillon's on her face.

"Abby's a likable person," he said, taking the wet plate his sister handed him and swiping the towel over it. "She's a good neighbor. Not like that guy who lived next to us when we shared that brownstone back in Chicago. The guy who was always stealing the paper. What was his name?"

"Mr. Quinlan, and stop trying to change the subject."

He stacked the plate with the others he'd already dried. "Don't make more of this than there is."

She pulled the stopper on the drain and leaned her hip against the sink. "Don't make less of this than there is," she countered softly. "I see the way you look at her."

He tossed down the towel, struggling for patience. "You know better than anyone why I'm not going down that path. I'm not cut out for it."

"Because you think you're too much like Dad was, or because of what happened with Maria?"

Trust his twin not to mince words.

"Just drop it." He turned to leave.

But she grabbed his arm. "I put my life on hold for five years for you," she reminded him tartly. "I gave up the only home I'd ever had until then and moved from Chicago to Weaver—started over *again*—just to satisfy your overprotective nature while you wormed your way into the Deuces."

"I get it. I owe you. I'm here, aren't I? I'm trying. I warned you I wouldn't be any good at it."

She gave a huge sigh. "Sloan, you don't *owe* me. I love you. I want to see you happy. And you know that my coming to Weaver turned out to be the best thing that ever happened to me, because this is where I found Axel. Why can't you just be hopeful? Go with your emotions for once?"

"Emotions never managed to get me anywhere I wanted to be."

"That's the past," she reminded him softly. "Abby's not Maria. Working for Max is not the same as pretending to be in league with a bunch of criminals. You lived long enough in the shadows. We did it when we were growing up because we had no choice, but things are different now. We're different."

"Are we?" He jerked his chin toward the window over the sink. "You're living exactly the sort of life you always dreamed of having."

"What sort of life did *you* dream of having?"

He chucked her lightly under the chin. "We're twins, Goob, but we're pretty damn different. *I* didn't dream."

She just shook her head. "Everyone has a dream. And you're only hurting yourself by pretending otherwise." She dried her hands. "And I still like Abby."

He stifled a curse. "She's too young."

Tara laughed at that. "She's raising a seven-year-old boy. She bought a house on her own, has an education and a good job. What she is is a young woman making a life for herself. She's not someone you need to rescue, and *that* is what probably scares the daylights out of you. Means you don't get to call all the shots and try to control everything. For the majority of us, that's what real life is." She patted his arm as she headed for the back door, grabbing a jacket off a hook on the way. "Whether Abby is in your future or not is up to the two of you. Just don't let what's happened in the past make the decision for you."

It took all of Abby's self-control not to watch Sloan too carefully when he followed his sister outside to join the football game.

Of course calling it a *football game* was playing fast and loose with the term. There *was* a football, and there did seem to be some sort of scoring. But mostly it was just a chance to run off too much pizza and—according to Chloe's father, Ryan—wear out the kids well enough that they went to sleep on time for once.

The success of which was proven later when Dillon dozed off on the drive home.

When they got to her house, Sloan offered to carry him inside for her.

"Thanks." She went ahead of him to unlock the door and then followed him down the hall to Dillon's room. She'd managed to keep her emotions in check since she'd waded into Sloan's sister's family and began introducing herself as if everything were perfectly normal.

But watching him settle her little brother so carefully in his bed now was more than she could take.

She turned on her heel and went out to the kitchen, kicking off her boots along the way. Needing something to do, she filled the coffee maker and started it up. The caffeine would keep her awake later, but it seemed smarter than pulling out the margarita mix left over from poker night with the girls. After those margaritas, she'd made out with Sloan in the middle of her front yard.

And look where that had led. He'd kissed her only to end up pushing her away.

She heard him when he came out from the bedroom but couldn't bring herself to look at him. "I'm making coffee." She stated the obvious. "Would you like some?"

"I'm sorry about all that crap at Tara's."

"We had a very nice time. Dillon particularly. Did you see him and Chloe? Like two peas in a pod."

"About *us*," he said.

As if she didn't know. "They were just poking at you the way families do." She pulled a mug from the cabinet and held it up. "Yes or no?"

He sat down on one of the barstools, tossing his leather jacket onto the empty stool beside him.

She took that as a yes and set the mug in front of him then got down a second one for herself. The scent of coffee was starting to fill the room, but the coffee maker still had plenty of gurgling to get through before it would be finished.

Which left her with nothing to keep herself busy, so she opened the container of cookies and set it on the counter. They were left over from the second batch she'd made, most of which had gone to Mr. Gilcrest next door.

"Dillon's shiner is really coming in."

She snatched up a cookie and broke off a corner, trying to keep her eyes from him. It was hard when he looked so darned good. "It's nothing to sound so pleased about. Calvin's is equally awful. It's no wonder his mother could barely stand talking to me."

He hesitated for a moment. "How was your grandmother when you visited today?"

She had the sense that hadn't been what he'd wanted to say. She plucked a paper napkin from the holder next to the toaster, folded it in half and set her cookie on it. "The same."

"Which means what?"

She sighed. "That she usually thinks I'm one of the nurses who works there and that Dillon is the grandson of the janitor."

"That's rough."

She chewed the inside of her lip and lifted her shoulders. "Thinking about it makes me want to cry," she admitted, "so I'd just as soon not think about it." Tears burned behind her eyes anyway.

"How long has she been sick?"

She turned to face the coffee maker, wishing the thing would hurry. "She was diagnosed six years ago. My grandfather took care of her, though, until he—" Her throat tightened. The machine spit out its last gasp of coffee, and she grabbed the pot, turning to fill Sloan's cup. "He had a massive heart attack two years ago."

"Then who took care of her?"

"I did at first."

"Weren't you still in nursing school?"

She nodded. "I hired someone for the days that I couldn't be there because of school. She watched Grandma, and then one of our neighbors helped get Dillon to and from school."

"Couldn't have been easy."

"That's just the way it was. My grandfather was always a planner and he'd planned well. Their house was paid for, plus there was insurance. In his will he made it plain that he wanted me to have guardianship of Dillon." Her throat tightened again. "And to do whatever I needed where my grandmother was concerned. He didn't want me feeling guilty when the day came that I wouldn't be able to care for her anymore. He'd already made arrangements for where she would go. Braden Bridge is a wonderful place."

"He sounds like quite a guy," he said after a moment. "What'd he do?"

"High-school math teacher. My grandmother was pretty great, too. This is her favorite cookie recipe, by the way. She was as quick with a kiss as she was a kick in the butt if she thought you needed one. I never once felt like I'd missed out on not having a mom. They loved me so much. I want Dillon to grow up feeling that same sense of security."

He nudged her fingers away from the handle of the coffeepot and filled her mug, since she'd clearly forgotten to. "Why wouldn't he?"

"That fight with Calvin doesn't shout success. He's never done such a thing at home in Braden, and we've barely settled in here, and *wham*."

"How often did he have nightmares in Braden?" he challenged. "Damn, but these things are good," he murmured, taking another cookie for himself and popping it into his mouth whole. He shoved the long sleeves of his dark gray T-shirt up his sinewy forearms. "You've only been here a few weeks. You can't judge anything by that."

"Maybe. I just don't want my decision to move here to have been a mistake." She pressed her fingertip into the crumbs from her cookie and absently sucked off the chocolate.

His sudden stillness penetrated the air, and she realized he was looking at her mouth.

"You haven't made a mistake." His voice was deeper than usual. His gaze jerked up to meet hers as if he'd realized where his focus had been.

Or maybe that was her imagination again, working overtime where he was concerned.

"You're in a new job," he continued, sounding a little gruff. "He's in a new school. You've both had a lot of changes, and that might make it rocky at first, but that'll smooth out in time."

She dabbed more crumbs onto her fingertip, only to wipe them off again on the napkin when she realized her hand was trembling. "Comforting words from a guy who can't commit to anything beyond the next few months."

His eyes narrowed slightly. "Sweet Abby Marcum has claws."

She blew out a noisy breath and shook her head. "Not really." She wiggled her spread fingers. "Just an occasional tendency to say inappropriate things. My grandfather used to call it my smart-i-tude."

He caught her fingers in his hands, and she froze. "If there's anything inappropriate around here, it's me."

She made a face, prepared to deny it. But her words

dried when he guided her fingertip back to the crumbled cookie and slowly pressed down, picking up crumbs the same way that she had. And when he pulled her finger to his mouth and closed his lips over the tip, her throat closed altogether.

Then he turned her hand, spreading her fingers flat, and kissed her palm.

Shivers danced down her spine. Something was working overtime inside her, and it definitely was not her imagination. "Sloan." It was barely a whisper.

His eyes looked into hers. "Inappropriate."

She swallowed hard. "Why? Are you hiding a wife somewhere after all?"

"I'm trying to be serious here, sweetheart."

But his lips had twitched again, so she grew a little braver. She'd encouraged Dee to open Joe Gage's eyes. Why shouldn't she try her own advice? She leaned her elbows on the counter, bringing herself closer to him, and turned her hand in his to slide her palm slowly against his. His eyes narrowed and he drew in a slow, careful breath.

The reaction made her feel heady.

"Do you actually have fuzzy aliens living in your attic?" she whispered seriously.

He waited a beat before chuckling softly. "You do make me laugh."

"Is that all?"

His jaw canted to one side. His eyes met hers again, and she felt the impact right down to her toes.

"We've already established that isn't all."

"And *that's* inappropriate. The fact that I—" She pressed her tongue against the edge of her teeth, steadying herself for a moment. "That you—"

"Yeah," he murmured. *"That."*

She leaned even closer, unintentionally crushing what was left of her cookie. She barely noticed. "Why?"

"You know why."

She slowly shook her head. "All you said was I didn't need a man like you."

"You're confusing the stories from the news with reality."

"I'm not confused." She inched closer until her lips were so close to his that she could feel the warmth of his breath on them. "I think you feel safer thinking that I'm confused."

He pulled back a few inches, one eyebrow lifting. "Is that a fact."

Her heart beat so hard in her chest, she felt dizzy from it. "It's not the guy in the news who built a snowman with my brother," she whispered. "Who gives him a ride on his motorcycle and encourages him. It's *you*. Dillon doesn't even know about what you did with the Deuces." His hero worship would know no bounds once he did.

"I'm not doing anything that anybody else wouldn't do," Sloan dismissed. "He's a good kid."

"He is," she agreed. "But you're wrong thinking everyone would treat him the same as you do. Just because I didn't leave behind a boyfriend in Braden doesn't mean I didn't have the opportunity."

His gaze sharpened. "What sort of opportunity?"

"Nothing I cared to explore. Not every guy has the patience to put up with having a little boy around." She shrugged. "And I don't have any interest in someone who doesn't understand how important Dillon is to me." Because she couldn't resist, she traced her thumb over his lower lip. "No matter what you say, you'll never make me believe you're not a good man."

"I want to sleep with you."

Her breath eked out. "I want to sleep with you, too," she managed to say, striving for calm and falling shudderingly short.

His gaze roved over her face, hesitating on her lips. "Just sex," he added flatly. "It's not about anything else but that. Still think I'm a good deal?"

Something about the way he said it penetrated her lightheadedness. His eyes were pinning her in place, oddly remote and divulging nothing in return.

This is the man who convinced a horde of thugs he was one of them.

The realization calmed her, and her hand shook only a little as she laid her palm along his jaw then trailed her fingertips down the hard column of his neck to the swirling edge of his tattoo, feeling him stiffen when she touched him there. "It's not going to work," she warned. "You won't scare me off by pretending you don't care." Then, before she lost her nerve, she leaned forward and brushed her mouth slowly over his.

Again.

And again.

Until she felt his lips soften, and he made a low sound that danced across her nerve endings. Then he moved suddenly, his fingers sliding through her hair, twisting gently as he pulled her head back.

The gaze that burned over her face was anything but remote. She didn't know what he was looking for, but he must have found it, because he gave that low groan again that thrilled her and fastened his mouth over hers. Hot. Hard. Deep.

She leaned closer, trying to wrap her arms around him, but the counter was in the way, and he seemed to realize it about the same time she did, because his hands left her hair and slid beneath her arms, and he pulled her right up onto the narrow surface.

She gasped.

"Don't wake your brother." He pushed aside the coffee mugs and the container of cookies. "Pull your legs over."

She shifted onto her rear, swung her legs around until she was sitting on top of the counter and tried not to gasp again when he closed his hands around her ankles and tugged her across the smooth surface until her chest hit his. Her heart raced and she was so afraid he'd stop that she caught her legs around his hips.

His expression turned unholy. "Have some experience with kitchen counters, do you?"

Her mouth opened; she almost blurted that she had no experience with anything at all, but he took advantage of her parted lips, kissing her again, even more deeply. And then she couldn't think about anything at all. Couldn't worry. Couldn't plan.

She could only feel.

Feel the heat of his fingers sliding beneath her sweater, slowly dragging it upward. He pulled away from their kiss so he could work the sweater over her head and toss it aside. Her own fingers flexed, desperate to get their own skin time, but his lips touched the side of her neck then burned their way down to her heartbeat that pulsed madly inside her chest.

Her head swam, and her hands fisted in his hair as he dragged his mouth over the lacy cups of her bra, dipped a finger inside and slowly drew it down until an aching nipple sprang free for him to taste.

Heat streaked from that wet warmth surrounding her to her center and she jerked, biting back a groan.

He drew in a hissing breath and straightened again,

crushing her against him. She could feel his pounding heart almost as well as she could feel her own.

"Tell me you're on the pill, sweetheart." His voice rasped against her ear as he kissed her cheek. Her neck. "Because it's been a long time since I've needed to carry around a condom."

She froze.

She was a *nurse,* for crying out loud.

Why hadn't she thought this far ahead?

"I, uh, I—" She tried to speak, but her throat was too tight. Every nerve in her body felt perched on a jagged edge, ready to splinter. "No," she managed to say and moaned a little when his teeth grazed the point of her shoulder as he drew the strap of her bra over it.

At first she wasn't sure he'd even heard, but his roving hand slowly stopped. He lifted his head. His eyes were hooded, even darker than usual, and filled with heat. "Not on the pill? What do you use?"

"Nothing," she whispered.

His eyebrows rose.

"There was never a need," she added, feeling shaky inside. "Before." Why wasn't there a how-to book somewhere that gave tips for situations like this?

His hands went from her hips to press flat against the countertop on either side of her. His eyes searched hers. "Abby?" He said just her name, but the way he drew it out, there was a wealth of questions in it.

She could either let him come to his own conclusion or she could head straight in and admit it first.

"I didn't need the pill," she said huskily, "because I've never…never done this before."

And then she flinched as he let out an oath and let her go as if she'd suddenly grown horns.

Chapter Eleven

Sloan stared at Abby. "You're a virgin," he said flatly, wanting clarification even though he didn't really need it. He should have realized. Should have figured that her aura of innocence went deeper than the surface.

Her lips were swollen and red from his kisses; her hair tumbled around her bare shoulders; her breasts lifted rapidly against the lacy bra barely confining them. Then her lashes lowered, hiding the clouds that her gray eyes had become. "I'm sorry."

He raked his hand down his face and stifled another oath. He started to move away from the counter, only to stop. He was hard as hell but at least the counter provided some shield. "There's nothing wrong with being a virgin."

"Really?" She didn't look at him as she pushed off the counter and bent to retrieve her sweater. "Then why are you looking at me with such horror?"

"It's not horror. It's surprise." He turned his back on her

because watching her put on her sweater was torment. He wished he could rewind time and undo the past hour or so.

Hell, if he was wishing for the impossible, why not rewind the past ten years?

The devil on his shoulder laughed maliciously. *She'd have been thirteen.*

He blew out a long breath and slowly looked at her. Thankfully, the sweater was back in place. Now he only had the vision of her body underneath to torture him for the rest of his days. "The only one who should apologize here is me."

Her chin crumpled slightly, and he braced himself for tears. But they didn't come. "I think you *should,*" she said, angling her chin instead. "Stopping like that was…rude." A fresh tide of red flowed through her cheeks.

Not the reaction he'd expected. Nothing about Abby was turning out like he'd expected. "A little smart-i-tude, Abby?"

She lifted her shoulder, but she didn't lower her chin.

He knew better than to smile, but something inside him felt lighter. "I don't have any experience with women like you," he admitted slowly.

The shadows in her eyes—shadows he'd put there—flickered. "I don't have any experience with women like me, either."

The bark of laughter escaped him.

She pressed her soft lips together. She didn't look quite amused, but at least she didn't look as if she were going to cry. He wasn't sure he'd be able to take it if he made her cry.

"Why didn't you tell me?"

She lifted her hands. "It's not like it's a natural topic of conversation, and I never thought we'd—" She broke off and shook her head, looking away.

He let out a long breath. "We're not going to solve this problem tonight."

"Is that what my virginity is? A problem?"

"The lack of condoms is a problem," he said bluntly and watched the way her eyes widened.

Then he watched a swallow work down her slender throat and tried not to think about the way it felt pressing his mouth against her creamy skin and the pulse thundering beneath.

"You're not turned off?"

The devil on his shoulder was cackling so merrily he fell right off his perch. Sloan closed his hands around her hips and pulled her close, rocking her toward him. "Sweetheart, there is nothing about you that doesn't turn me *on*."

She inhaled audibly. Her hands roved over his shoulders, fingertips kneading. "I didn't mean to start something I couldn't finish," she whispered.

"I believe you. This is not your fault, so don't tell me you're sorry again." Then he kissed her. Well and thoroughly.

And when he couldn't take it another second, he set her from him. "That's a poor substitute for everything else I want," he said huskily, "but it's going to have to do for now."

"It's not a kiss-off?"

He shook his head, amused despite himself. "You don't have a clue what sort of hold you have over me, do you. Things are nowhere near finished, Abby. And next time, I can promise you I'll be prepared." He scooped up the two remaining cookies that had escaped their countertop antics and gave her a long look. "You won't have any reason to call me rude for stopping...*like that*."

Her eyes turned smoky.

Before he could lose his remaining sliver of self-control,

he grabbed his jacket and headed for the door. "Thanks for the cookies."

She just gave him a bemused look. "You're welcome."

Abby didn't catch a glimpse of Sloan the next morning. His SUV was already gone when she hustled Dillon out the door for school.

But that was okay. She knew she'd see him soon enough.

Things were working out.

Sloan hadn't looked at her as if she were a space alien when he'd learned she was a virgin. If he had cared about that, he wouldn't still want to see her.

It was all she could do not to grin like a buffoon when she left Dillon outside his classroom and headed to her office.

She hummed her way through three hours of vision screenings at the junior high, doodled through a conference call with the education board and realized she'd forgotten to pack her own lunch when Dee stopped by her office, brown bag in hand.

"Come and share my misery," Dee begged. "I have ten minutes to eat and then playground duty."

Abby chuckled. "It can't be *that* bad."

Dee clucked her tongue. "You really are young. The Pollyanna luster hasn't had a chance to wear off. Give it a few more years." She gestured. "You coming or not?"

Abby had nothing else she needed to take care of, and it was her lunch hour. "Why not?" She pushed away from her desk and retrieved her coat.

The lunch bell had rung, and the hall was filled with children boisterously leaving their classrooms behind. "You want to pick up something to eat from the cafeteria?" Dee asked over the chaos.

Who needed food? She was floating on air. "I'm fine."

They reached the heavy metal doors that led outside, and Dee gave her a sideways look. "It's a Monday, for God's sake. But you're even more chipper than usual. Why?"

She pushed open the door and led the way to the playground. "No reason."

Dee narrowed her eyes but didn't say anything until they reached one of the benches. So far, the space was quiet since the children were inside for lunch, and they sat down.

Abby stretched out her legs and lifted her face to the sun.

"Oh my God," Dee muttered softly. "Are you sleeping with Deputy Hottie?"

Abby jerked and stared at Dee. "What? No!"

Dee just pursed her lips knowingly. Her eyes danced. "Don't tell lies to your elders."

Abby rolled her eyes and looked away. "Give me a break."

"Well, *something* has gotten into you. If it's not your hot neighbor, who is it?"

"Dee!" Despite her embarrassment, Abby laughed. "Someone's going to hear you."

Dee made a point of looking around them at the entirely empty playground. "Come on. Dish."

"There's nothing to dish about!"

"He was bad in the sack, huh?" Dee tsked. "Well, just because a guy looks great doesn't always mean he'll *be* great. Learned that lesson a time or two myself."

Abby covered her face, shaking her head. "Too much information, Dee."

Her friend laughed. Then she bumped her shoulder against Abby's. "So it *was* good, then."

She flushed and looked away. "I'm not going to talk about this with you."

"Oh, come on." Dee's laughter died away, but she was still amused. "You really like him?"

She nodded. "I do."

"Oh, well, shoot," Dee grumbled. "Now I'm *really* jealous. Although, the next poker night won't be so costly if you're not among us spinsters."

"None of you are spinsters," Abby said with a laugh. "I still can't believe you call yourselves that."

"Honey, most of us are over thirty and not a one of us is tied up with a man." Dee's expression turned devilish. "Rope ties being the exception."

"Dee!"

"Just kidding. It is *way* too easy to shock you." Dee looked over her shoulder to make sure that the doors to the school building were still closed. "So is it serious? This thing between you and Sloan?"

Abby thought about it. "I don't know."

"Has he decided to stay in town after all?"

"I don't know," she said again. And she didn't really want to think about it because when she did, it had a particularly dampening effect on the happiness bubbling inside her.

"Not that there's anything wrong with just enjoying the moment," Dee added. "As long as you know that's what you're doing."

She knew that Dee was trying to watch out for her. "I know."

Dee studied her for a moment. Then her eyes filled with mischief again. "I'm still jealous."

Abby laughed, and soon, the metal doors behind them clanged. Children spewed out into the sunshine, propelled by a morning's worth of cooped-up energy.

Dee put aside her lunch on the bench. "Brace yourself,"

she warned, pushing herself to her feet. "Now the real fun of the day begins."

Abby rose, too, even though she had no particular responsibility as a playground monitor the way the teachers who shared the job in rotating shifts did. Dee wasn't alone, either; she was soon joined by Rob Rasmussen, the teacher who'd caught Dillon and Calvin fighting in the bathroom. Two of the student teachers whose names Abby couldn't recall came out to supervise, as well.

She wandered among the children as they clustered in their obviously familiar groups. Some headed off onto the snowy baseball field, some climbed on the jungle-gym equipment and some sat huddled on the cement pads that were painted with lines for activities. She tossed a bouncing red ball back to a foursome of chattering little girls and spotted Dillon and Chloe Clay heading for the swing set.

When the bell rang a half hour later, Abby felt almost as much disappointment as the kids did. She returned to her office and a ringing phone, which she grabbed as she shrugged out of her coat. "Nurse's office."

"Do nurses ever wear white uniforms and caps anymore?"

Pleasure flooded her at the sound of Sloan's voice, and she smiled as if he were there to see it. "Is your fantasy showing, Deputy?"

He laughed softly. "Might bear some thinking about."

She very nearly shivered. She glanced at her empty doorway as she sat down behind her desk. "How do you feel about sturdy white shoes with rubber soles that squeak against the floors?"

"Now whose freak is showing?"

She giggled. The only fantasy she had was *him;* hearing his voice was enough to have her squirming in her chair. "How's your day been?"

"Long. One of the other deputies is going to be out for a while. Ruiz. He had an emergency appendectomy yesterday."

"That's too bad. Is he all right?"

"He will be. But I have to take his spot at a conference in Cheyenne. Leaving this afternoon."

Disappointment swamped her. Then she shook herself. He was just doing his job. "How long will you be gone?"

"We'll be back on Friday."

"Who else is going?"

"Max and Dawson."

She ignored a quick jab of jealousy. Dawson, the one who jogged in the park and never wimped out. "What's the conference about?"

"It's a national thing once a year. Combined agencies, a bunch of workshops. Ruiz's appendectomy is a pain in my ass," he added wryly. "I hate sitting in meetings."

"Maybe you'll learn something valuable."

"Maybe I'll be thinking about you in a cute little nurse's cap and nothing else."

He laughed softly when she caught her breath, and she knew he'd said it just to shock her. "Maybe I'll be waiting for you on Friday wearing exactly that," she managed to say smoothly and enjoyed the way he choked a little on his laughter. "I'll miss you," she admitted.

"Find someone to watch Dillon Friday night."

Her stomach swooped, and her mind seemed to fizz. "Okay." A movement at her doorway had her sitting up straight, though. "Thank you for calling," she added primly.

His laughter was low and knowing. "Friday, sweetheart." Then he hung up.

She swallowed, trying to look at least vaguely professional as she replaced the phone and gestured for the student who was clutching a hall pass to enter.

That student was the first in a stream of them, not leaving Abby with a lot of time to dwell on the call. She made up for it that night, though, after Dillon was sound asleep, and she couldn't close her eyes without images of Sloan overwhelming her.

But even that was okay, she realized, as she turned her head into her pillow. Because she went to sleep and dreamed of him.

The next day, after Abby left Dillon at his classroom she headed to Dee's room. Her friend made her way around the children hanging up their coats and met Abby in the doorway. "What's up?"

"Can you watch Dillon for me Friday night?"

Dee's eyebrows went up. "Deputy Hottie?"

Abby rolled her eyes, but she couldn't very well deny it. And there wasn't much time before the final bell would ring, signaling the start of classes. "Try not to announce it to the world, okay? So can you?"

Dee grinned. "Sure. Second and thirds get dismissed late that day, you know. Because of the Cee-Vid field trip."

Abby wanted to slap her head for forgetting. "I already told Dillon he couldn't go because of that fight." She shifted to allow a little girl lugging a backpack that was half her size to get past.

"He'll probably be the only one not going," Dee said seriously. "The tour is one of the highlights of the year." The bell buzzed over the last of her words, and she looked over her shoulder. "Seats," she called out, and the kids began scrambling. "Just think about it," she told Abby as she reached for the door and started to close it. "Either way, you can count on me for Friday night." She grinned quickly. "But if it spills over onto Saturday morning, I've got a pole-dancing fitness class at eleven."

Abby tried not to choke on her laughter as she stepped into the hall so that Dee could close the door. All up and down the corridor, she could hear the similar sound of other doors closing, and then she was alone, and the sudden silence nearly echoed.

She turned on her heel, and the sole of her shoe squeaked loudly on the tile.

She hurried to her own office, where she wouldn't be caught grinning like a fool.

"Sheriff's looking for you."

Stifling a yawn, Sloan glanced up from the report he was reading on trends in crime in rural areas to kill time between conference sessions. "Where is he, Dawson?"

"Coffee shop."

Glad for a reason to move, he handed the dull report to her. "Better than prescription sleep aids."

She eyed the thick report ruefully. "I'll bet." She tucked it in her bag. "See you at dinner." Without a second glance, she headed off as he worked his way through the crowded hotel lobby to the coffee shop. It, too, was teeming with conference attendees, but Sloan spotted Max easily enough and wound his way through the tables to reach him.

"What's up?"

Max gestured toward the chair opposite him. "Glad you're here. Gives me a chance to talk to you for a second."

They'd been in Cheyenne since the previous afternoon. Max had had ample opportunities to talk to Sloan if he'd wanted. "About?"

"Your plans." Max stuck his mug out for the harried-looking waitress, and she splashed coffee into it without slowing her stride. "If you've been thinking about the offer I made."

"I've been thinking," Sloan allowed. "You in a hurry for an answer all of a sudden?"

Max toyed with the coffee mug. "Do I need to sweeten the pot?"

Sloan grimaced. "I'm not angling for anything, Max. I just don't know if—"

"—if you want to stay in Weaver." His boss's fingers flicked off the idea. "You've been clear about that from the start." He glanced toward the door. "I need a chief deputy."

Sloan went still. "Ruiz has the most seniority. He'll be back on his feet before long."

"It's not a matter of seniority. In any case, Ruiz has already told me he's not interested. Doesn't want the stress."

Sloan snorted. "Does anyone?" The chief deputy would be second in line only to the sheriff. "How much is administrative?"

"Not as much as I've got to deal with."

"I don't have the experience."

Max snorted.

Sloan shifted. "Supervisory experience," he added.

"A man's gotta start somewhere." He glanced toward the door again. He didn't seem to see what he was looking for and sat forward. "I have to get my butt reelected every four years. But I get to hire who I want. And I want you."

"Why?"

"Because you're good at what you do," Max said bluntly. "I know the job is a helluva lot more staid than running undercover with the Deuces, but it's still important. The department covers a lot of territory. Lot of people count on us."

"Why'd *you* decide to make the change?" Sloan knew that Max's history was with the DEA.

The older man's lips twitched slightly. "Sarah."

Max was talking about his wife. But it was Abby who popped into Sloan's head way too easily.

Then his boss glanced at the door again and muttered an oath. "Just keep it in mind, okay?"

Sloan frowned but nodded. And then he stiffened when he recognized the man approaching them.

Max had risen, his hand extended to the other man. "Sean. Good to see you again." He gestured toward Sloan. "I agreed to get him here because I owed you one. Now we're even." He tossed a few bucks down on the table for the waitress as he stepped out of the way. "Deputy Mc-Cray." He pinned Sloan with a look. "We'll finish this later."

Sloan nodded once, but he didn't look away from the interloper's face. He did wait, however, until his boss had walked away before he let his feelings show. "Didn't know the ATF was sending special agents all the way out here from the Chicago field office," he drawled. "Or are you just slumming, Sean?"

Sean Cowlings smiled thinly. "Good to know there's still no love lost between us." He took the seat that Max had vacated, pushed aside the thick white coffee mug and folded his manicured hands on top of the table. "Think you're the one slumming it. You happy playing traffic cop in the middle of nowhere?"

He let the insult slide. He and Sean had come up in the academy together, but to say they'd been friends would have been seriously overstating it. "What do you want?" There wasn't any question that Sean had maneuvered to see Sloan. Max had made that clear.

Sean smoothed his hand down his silk tie. "We've got intel that Tony Diablo is trying to reestablish the Deuces."

Sloan's jaw tightened. "Tony's a punk. He'll never succeed at replacing his cousin."

Sean shrugged, not giving away whether he agreed. "I'm in charge of the investigation. ASAC."

Assistant Special Agent in Charge. Old Seany-boy had been promoted. "You always did have your eye on the ladder."

"You're in a unique position to understand all the pieces where the Deuces are concerned."

"The Deuces don't exist anymore," Sloan said flatly. "Without Johnny, it's a dead deal."

"Johnny's dead, too."

Sloan looked away. He'd known about the man's death in a prison fight. The day after he'd heard the news, he'd decided to give Weaver a try. "What's your point, Sean? I've got a gripping seminar on internet crime to get to."

"We want you back."

Sloan laughed. "As what? You running confidential informants?" He couldn't exactly go undercover anymore. His face had seen too much airtime.

"Officially," Sean clarified. He looked none too pleased at the attention Sloan's bark of laughter had garnered. "Full benefits as if you'd never left."

Sloan's laughter dried up. "I didn't choose to leave," he reminded him flatly. "I was escorted out the door by an armed guard."

"Standard procedure."

"Screw standard procedure." He wanted to say it much more bluntly, but there was a little kid who reminded him of Dillon sitting with his dad on the other side of the aisle. "The agency treated me like I was an embarrassment at the least and a freaking criminal at the worst."

Sean's lips thinned. "And they were wrong. You think *I* wanted to be the one sent to deliver their mea culpa?"

"You've always been someone's lackey, Sean." Sloan pushed to his feet. He'd had more than enough of the man's company. "If it weren't for you, they'd have never known I'd made my private deal with Hollins-Winword to protect Maria and my sister. The suits would have never been able to use that as an excuse to fire me."

"You broke protocol," Sean said tightly. "You knew it and you did it anyway."

"Damn straight," he said flatly. "And I'd do it again in a second." He turned on his heel and began working his way out of the restaurant.

"Like it or not, McCray—" Sean's voice followed him "—nobody can stop Tony better than you. You'll never be able to walk away from that!"

Chapter Twelve

"How was your day?"

When she heard Sloan's voice, Abby tucked the phone against her shoulder and sat up in bed. "It's nearly midnight."

"Were you sleeping?"

"Yes."

"Dreaming?"

She smiled into the darkness. "Yes."

"About what?"

She curled her bare toes into the sheets. "Something very…naughty."

"You've never been naughty in your life."

"A person's gotta start somewhere. Why not in their dreams?"

He gave a low laugh. "What was it? Leaving school fifteen minutes before you're supposed to?"

Her smile widened. "Riding on the back of your motorcycle, actually."

"Now I know you're screwing with me."

She tucked her chin over her drawn-up knees. She wasn't about to tell him that it had been vividly erotic having her arms clutched around his rigid midriff with the throaty engine rumbling beneath them. "My day was an entirely ordinary Tuesday," she said, answering his original question. "Finished up vision screenings with the junior-high kids this morning. Then back to my office for two fevers and an asthma attack. What about you? Learning anything fascinating?"

"Learning that sitting on my butt watching PowerPoint presentations is no more interesting than it ever was. How's Dillon?"

"He's nearly done with the poster he wants to enter in the sheriff's contest. He asked if Chloe could come home with us from school tomorrow to play 'White Hats.' I said she could."

"What is this whole White Hat thing, anyway?"

"Video game. His favorite." She told him the premise behind the game.

"And he wants to play it now with Chloe Clay. Romance is starting younger every day."

She laughed softly. "I'm not going to worry about that unless I see him deliberately losing the game to her."

"You get him taken care of for Friday night?"

She hadn't expected that he'd forget, but having him mention it sent excitement through her. "Yes."

"Good. Then I'll get everything else taken care of."

She could only imagine what that meant. "Okay."

"Sorry I waked you."

"I'm not."

He was silent for a moment. She imagined him smiling slightly. Hoped he would be, anyway.

"I wish you were here, though," she added.

"Get some sleep, Abby." His voice deepened. "I wish I were there, too," he added before he hung up.

She was smiling when she fell back asleep to dream, yet again, of Sloan.

She was still smiling the next day, until Calvin Pierce appeared in her office doorway clutching a hall pass. The bruise beneath his eye was fading, but it still stood out against his pale skin just like Dillon's did.

She gestured him inside. "Calvin? Are you sick?"

He shook his head and continued hovering in front of her desk. He looked around to see if anyone was in the back part of her office where two cots were positioned, and his shoulders seemed to fall when he saw that they were both occupied. "Are they sick?"

"Fevers." The flu had begun making its annual rounds. "They're waiting for their parents to come and pick them up." She pulled the sliding door between the rooms nearly closed and rounded her desk to press her hand against Calvin's forehead. It was little-boy warm, but nothing worse. "What's wrong?"

He angled away from her. "Ms. Normington said I hadda come and get a bandage." He held up his hand, showing her a wicked gash on his palm.

"Sit down." She nudged him onto one of the chairs in front of her desk before going to her sink to wash her hands. "How'd you get the cut?" When he didn't answer, she looked over her shoulder at him. "Calvin?"

He hunched his shoulders. "My dad broke sump'n."

It wasn't exactly a detailed explanation.

She dried her hands and pulled out supplies to clean him up, too, since there was no point in bandaging the wound if his hands were still filthy. She sat down next to him with gauze and antiseptic wash and spread a clean towel over her lap before taking his hand and spreading it flat. "How's your eye feeling?"

"Fine." He didn't even flinch when she carefully washed his hand and irrigated the cut, though she knew it had to sting. He thumped the front of her metal desk rhythmically with his tennis shoe.

She studied him as she worked. His clothes were shabby and worn, but they were clean. His socks were mismatched, and his tennis shoes barely had soles left. She remembered how his coat had been two sizes too small when she'd spoken to his mother and him outside Ruby's.

She finished cleaning his hand then calmly began working on his wrist, which was covered in fading bruises.

"Did you cut yourself this morning?"

"Last night."

She'd suspected as much, just from the state of the wound. "No bandages at home?"

He looked down again. Shook his head.

The sight of two violently purple finger-sized bruises on the back of his neck made her close her eyes. She had to hold back a shudder.

"Well," she managed to say, though her throat felt tight. "We'll take care of that now." She dried his hand and taped it up then dropped some supplies into a plastic bag that she gave to him. "You can take those with you," she said. "You have to keep the cut clean and covered, or it might get infected."

"So?"

He was the little bully of the school. He'd been tormenting Dillon from day one. But she still wanted to pull him close and hug away his hurt.

Because there was no doubt in her mind that he was definitely hurt.

"It takes longer to heal if it gets infected," she said smoothly. She signed his hall pass and returned it to him. "Go back to your class, Calvin."

He took the pass and turned to leave.

"Calvin?"

He looked over his shoulder. "What?"

"Everything's going to be okay."

"Whatever," he muttered as he left.

She realized she was shaking and badly wished that she could call Sloan.

She cleaned up the supplies and checked on the students still resting before she went next door. "Mrs. Timms, would you mind waiting in my office for a few minutes? I have two students whose parents are supposed to pick them up anytime now, and I need to speak with Principal Gage."

Mrs. Timms gave her a look brimming with disapproval. "Principal Gage is a very busy man."

She peered at the older woman. "And it's imperative that I speak with him *now*," she said flatly. "Are you willing to go next door and supervise my office for a few minutes or not?"

"Abby?" Joe appeared in his doorway. "What's going on?"

Tears were burning behind her eyes, but she was damned if she was going to let them fall and prove how unequipped she was for the job for which she'd been hired. "I need to talk to you about C-Calvin."

His brows pulled together. He extended his arm. "Viola. Go next door."

The woman sniffed, clearly put out, but she rose and swept past Abby into the hall.

"Come on in," Joe said.

Swallowing hard, Abby entered his office and waited until he'd closed the door. "Someone is beating Calvin Pierce." Just saying the words nearly choked her. "I'd bet my license on it."

He nudged her onto a chair and pushed a box of tissues toward her. "How do you know?"

She grabbed a tissue, but she was too upset to sit, so she stood up and paced around the office as she told him about Calvin's cut. "He has old bruises on his wrist. And yes—" she looked at the principal "—I know kids get bruises for a host of perfectly innocent reasons. Dillon's usually sporting a variety of them himself." She bunched the tissue in her fist. "But it's pretty hard to get a pair of fingerprints on the back of one's neck by accident, and that's what I just saw on Calvin!" Her breath shuddered out of her. She held up her hand, fingers spread. "The bruises were twice the size of my fingers, Joe. An adult did that."

He exhaled, swearing ripely. "Sorry."

She shook her head. "Nothing I don't want to say myself." She pressed her lips together. "I have to report it to the sheriff."

"Yes. You do." He looked grim. "This'll likely get worse before it gets better, but Calvin's the important one."

She nodded and waited while he picked up the phone and made the call. It took only a few minutes before he was done. "They're sending over an officer now."

"Have, uh, have you ever had this happen before?"

"Once." He ran his hand over his thinning hair. "And that was one time too many." He looked out the window behind his desk. "They'll take your report. Get one from me and likely Olivia Normington, as well. Someone from protective services will come and talk to Calvin. His parents will be interviewed. They'll make the determination whether Calvin is in immediate danger."

"Would there be any doubt?" Her voice rose again. She raked back her hair, composing herself. "Sorry. It's just—"

"—upsetting. I should have seen something before now."

"If it weren't for Mrs. Normington sending him to me because of his cut, I wouldn't have seen anything, either."

"Crazy to be grateful a kid got a cut on his hand," he muttered.

A few minutes later, one of the deputies from the sheriff's office arrived, and Joe left them alone in his office so Abby could make her report.

By the end of the day, the entire school buzzed with the news that the sheriff's department had been there and that little Calvin Pierce had been taken away by a lady in a suit who'd come all the way from Gillette.

"Hey." Dee came by Abby's office just as she was closing it up for the day. "How're you doing?"

She dropped her keys in her purse. "What's a little exhaustion compared to what Calvin's going through?" She shook her head. "Who knows how long it's been happening."

"I heard Viola Timms was bawling her eyes out in the bathroom," Dee murmured. "Guess she has a heart lurking in her skinny chest after all."

"Everyone's upset." They turned in unison and walked toward the exit. Abby knew that Dillon would already be outside waiting for her, Chloe undoubtedly with him, since those particular plans hadn't changed just because Calvin's world had been tilted off its axis. "Have you ever had to make a report like that?"

Dee shook her head and tucked her arm through Abby's. "You call Sloan and tell him?"

"Yes." He hadn't been able to talk long. Just sighed when he heard the news and asked if she was okay.

"Who took the report?"

"Jerry Cooper. Do you know him?"

"Yeah." Dee smiled, though the news about Calvin had dimmed her spirit, too. "He pulled me over for speeding once. Besides that he's okay." She pushed open the exit door. "Call me if you want company tonight," she said before turning toward the parking lot.

Dillon and Chloe were waiting exactly where they were supposed to be, and his eyes were wide. "Calvin got *arrested*," he told her.

"He wasn't arrested," she corrected and smiled at Chloe. The little girl was cute as could be with her brown hair pulled up in pigtails and her blue eyes as bright as buttons. "You ready to play some 'White Hats'?"

Chloe's pigtails bobbed as she nodded. She grabbed Dillon's hand then grabbed Abby's with her other. "I'm ready to *win* some 'White Hats.'"

"You're not gonna win," Dillon scoffed, tugging his hand away to wipe it on the front of his coat.

And for the first time since that morning, Abby felt a real smile tug at her lips.

Romance indeed.

She flipped his hood up so it fell over his nose. "You can go on the field trip on Friday," she said.

His jaw dropped a little.

Then he let out a whoop and grabbed Chloe's hand. They jogged ahead, their backpacks bouncing.

Thankfully, the rest of the week passed without any additional traumas, and the mood at the school settled some.

By the end of the day on Friday, Abby locked up her office with indecent haste the second she could.

Dee had agreed to drive Dillon home when their classes returned from the field trip and then stay there with him while Abby and Sloan did…whatever. Which left Abby with about an hour and a half of entirely free time, and she didn't intend to waste a moment of it.

She practically jogged home and tossed her briefcase on her bedroom dresser. She let Rex out long enough to do his business then gave him a dog biscuit, grabbed her keys and closed the door on his imploring face. She drove downtown to Classic Charms, which according to Dee was "the" place to shop for anything decent in Weaver. The fact that the shop was owned by Sloan's sister couldn't be helped. Not that Abby didn't like Tara. She did. But she didn't necessarily want to shop for something pretty to wear for Sloan under the knowing eye of his twin sister.

But Tara wasn't there anyway. A friendly girl who looked a few years younger than Abby was manning the old-fashioned cash register, and she was happy to direct Abby through the eclectic shop to the women's clothing.

She quickly rummaged through the hangers, wishing she had more time to go through the plethora of unusually nice things. It was certainly a better selection than what she'd ever find out at Shop-World. She grabbed a long, ivory cowl-necked sweater that she could pair with tights and boots, and dithered longer than she had time for over a display of outrageously priced, outrageously pretty panties only to pass on them all because every time she thought about wearing them—about Sloan *seeing* them—she lost her nerve.

She quickly paid for her purchases then raced back home and was glad that Jerry Cooper wasn't watching for speeders or she'd have been caught for sure. She showered in record time and was drying her hair when she heard the door open and Dillon's young voice yelling her name.

She tightened the belt of her robe and went out to greet

him. "Hey there!" He had a plastic bag clutched in his fist. "What do you have?"

"Video games," he said reverently and dumped them out right there on the hallway floor. "Everyone got a whole bag!"

"Exciting." Abby stepped around him to meet Dee as she came inside. "Thanks for bringing him back."

Dee's gaze ran over her. "If that's the attire for the evening, guess I don't have to ask what you'll be doing."

Abby flushed. "I have clothes."

Dee just grinned wickedly, and Abby was glad the other woman didn't pursue it. "How long before Deputy Ho— McCray gets here?"

"He said by six."

"Know what he has planned?"

She flushed even harder.

"Never mind," Dee said dryly. "I can figure that one out." She glanced at her watch. "I'm just gonna run back over to the school and grab some papers I need to grade. I'll be back in time."

"Thanks, Dee."

"What're spinster friends for?" She grinned and left.

Abby quickly looked over the games that Dillon had brought home, just to make certain they were appropriate for his age. "Sure you're okay with Ms. Crowder watching you this evening?"

He shrugged, clearly more interested in his bounty than either her or Rex, who was bouncing around trying to steal the discarded plastic bag. She roughed up Dillon's hair and hurried back into the bathroom to turn on the blow-dryer once more. As long as she focused on one thing at a time and didn't think too far ahead to what the evening would hold, she could function. More or less.

When she heard pounding on the front door a short

while later, she gulped. Not only was Sloan early, he sounded impatient. She dashed her hands down her robe again, hurried toward the front door and nearly jumped out of her skin when it crashed open before she could reach it.

Rex yipped and raced past the intruder's legs, bolting for freedom.

They weren't Sloan's legs.

A complete stranger was standing there, eyeing her with cold-blooded loathing. He pointed at her. "They took my boy 'cause of you."

Horrified realization rolled through her. She grabbed Dillon and pushed him behind her. "Go to your bedroom and lock the door," she ordered. "Now!"

Looking terrified, he scrambled down the hall, and she waited tensely until she heard the door slam. Then she eyed Bobby Pierce and completely, fully understood why Sloan had been so adamant that she keep her distance.

She edged toward the kitchen, wondering what her chances were of getting to her grandpa's shotgun before Bobby got to her and figuring they weren't stellar considering he was about as close to the kitchen as she was. "You shouldn't be here, Mr. Pierce."

"Why not?" He stepped farther into the house, eyeing her up and down. "Got no place else. Can't go home. Can't see my wife. Can't see my boy."

Thank God for that, she thought, but wisely didn't voice it. "Breaking in like this won't help your case to get them back."

"Wasn't locked."

"You entered without my permission." She sidestepped a little more. The breakfast counter was the problem. She had to go around it to get into the kitchen, which would take her closer to Pierce. "But if you open up that door again and leave now," she suggested reasonably, "we can forget this ever happened." *Like hell.*

He took a long step into the room, ending any hope she had of making it into the kitchen, and she changed course instantly, backing instead into the living room.

He smiled gruesomely, clearly pleased with her retreat, particularly when she had to stop abruptly because of the fireplace at her back. He advanced. "Afraid, little girl?"

Desperately.

"You're loathsome," she hissed. The iron fireplace poker felt wonderfully solid as she reached behind her and silently wrapped her hand around it. The closer he drew, the stronger the stench of liquor became. "Does it make you feel big and powerful to beat up a little boy?"

"You bitch." He raised a fist, and she braced herself, prepared to swing the poker. "You don't know nothing about me."

"She doesn't. But I do."

Abby's knees nearly went out from beneath her at the sound of Sloan's voice.

"Take another step, Bobby," he warned as he stepped through the front door. "Give me a reason to shoot you."

There was no question Sloan meant it.

The gun he was aiming at Pierce made that more than clear.

"Abby." His gaze never strayed an inch from the man he was watching with deadly calm. "Dillon's outside waiting for you. Go on now."

The fireplace poker clattered noisily as she dropped it and fled around Bobby, stopping only to snatch up her snow boots that were lying by the door before running outside.

Dillon was, indeed, standing next to Sloan's cruiser, huddled alongside Mr. Gilcrest. She shoved her feet into the boots and ran down the steps, not caring that she was wearing a robe and little else. She lifted Dillon in her arms, also not caring one whit if he thought he was too old and too big for such things. "You're supposed to be in your room!"

Her brother just hugged her tightly around her neck and hung on. She looked around, wondering where Rex had run off to, but didn't want to say anything. Dillon was already upset enough.

"Climbed out his window," Mr. Gilcrest offered by way of explanation. His lined face was proud. "Said you needed help." His words were drowned out by the screaming siren of a SUV like Sloan's. It stopped in front of Sloan's house, and two uniformed deputies quickly emerged. "Dep'ty Mc-Cray got here before I finished calling 911."

Abby rubbed Dillon's back. "You brave boy." She kissed his cheek and willed the other deputies to move faster. Sloan had a gun. But he was still in there alone with a crazy person.

The other neighbors were coming out onto their porches, venturing onto the street to see what the commotion was all about. One of the deputies who'd just arrived broke off and started waving at everyone to keep back. Abby buried her head against Dillon's, controlling the urge to scream at them all, because as long as the deputy was watching out for *them,* he couldn't watch out for Sloan.

"Everything's fine," she whispered to Dillon. "It's all going to be fine." She repeated it, again and again, like a litany.

Sloan waited until he was sure that Abby was gone before he spoke. "You are the dumbest son of a bitch to ever walk this earth, you know that, Bobby?"

The other man craned his head around, his lips twisted in contempt. "You're not gonna shoot me."

"Might." The image of Abby's terrified face wasn't going to leave him anytime soon, and it filled him with the kind of rage he'd never wanted to feel again. He lifted his firearm and sighted on Bobby's forehead only because he knew, even as angry as he was, he'd never pull the trigger. He didn't know what he was, but he wasn't a killer. Not anymore. "This close? No possible way of missing." His arm shifted and he aimed lower. "Course I could just shoot you somewhere else. Nobody'd care much if I gelded you."

The fool actually paled and took a faltering step back. "You wouldn't."

Moving faster than he remembered he could, Sloan holstered his weapon and slammed the man up against the brick fireplace, his arm on Bobby's windpipe. "Or I could just put you out of your misery like this," he gritted. "What d'you think, Bobby? You want to take me on? See what it's like with someone who isn't smaller?" He pressed a little harder, hearing Bobby wheeze. "Who isn't weaker?" He waited a beat. "I *ever* see you around Abby or Dillon again, I'll finish this," he promised. "You understand me?"

Bobby's eyes were filling with panic. His wheezing was coming harder, and his hands scrabbled against Sloan's immovable arm.

"You're going to leave Lorraine alone. And you're gonna leave Calvin alone. Got it?"

Bobby couldn't nod but he blinked furiously. Sloan figured it was close enough. He flipped him around and cuffed him while Bobby was still gasping for air.

"You're crazy," Bobby yelled hoarsely as Sloan searched him for weapons.

"Yeah. I was a Deuce, you jerk. We were all crazy." Finding nothing on the man but a thin wallet, Sloan shoved him toward the front door and pushed him out into the cold, where an indistinguishable streak of color flew at him. Rex growled and snapped at Bobby's legs, and the guy howled when the dog found some purchase. He kicked Rex off him, but the dog didn't back off. He continued snarling ferociously, and while it was tempting to let him go at Bobby again, Sloan didn't. "Rex, sit."

The dog's butt hit the porch deck. He whined once, watching Sloan hand Bobby over to Max, who must have just arrived.

"He tried to kill me," Bobby screamed as Max yanked him toward his waiting vehicle. "You gonna do anything about that?"

"Ask him why he didn't finish the job," Sloan heard his boss respond mildly.

Sloan wasn't interested in hearing anything more, though. He pulled off his coat and headed for Abby and Dillon, wrapping it around them before pulling them both into his arms. His throat felt tight, and his head was pounding the way it always had from too much adrenaline. "You okay?"

Abby nodded against him. Even though she was already holding Dillon in her arms, she managed to wind an arm around Sloan's neck, too. "Welcome home." She laughed thickly then promptly burst into tears.

He pressed his cheek to her head, wanting to kill Bobby all over again. He brushed back Dillon's hair until he could see the kid's eyes. They were still dilated with fear. He rubbed his thumb over the tears on Dillon's cheeks. "You're both pretty brave, you know that?"

"Is that man gonna be gone forever now?"

"I sure hope so, Dillon." Sloan slid his arm around the boy, taking his weight off of Abby as best he could, considering the awkwardness of their positions. He watched over their heads as Max drove off with Bobby. Pierce wouldn't be gone forever, he knew.

But maybe he'd be gone long enough that his family could find some peace.

Abby shifted. Her cheeks were wet, her eyes a drenched sea of gray. "So much for our Friday night, huh?"

The night wasn't going to end up anything like what he'd anticipated. But he couldn't care less.

"You're safe," he said roughly. "That's the only thing that I care about right now." Then he kissed her on the lips, not caring in the least what conclusions Dillon or anyone else who saw them would draw.

Chapter Thirteen

Even though Max had taken Bobby away, it wasn't long before it seemed as if half the town was crowding onto their short street.

Sloan took Abby and Dillon over to his place, since the idea of going back into their own house leached the color right back out of both their drawn faces.

"Get a little crowd control going," he suggested as they passed Jerry Cooper, who'd also arrived. Sloan managed not to yell the instruction, so he figured maybe he had more self-control left than he thought. Then he remembered Rex and gave a sharp whistle. The dog came running.

Once inside, he left Abby, Dillon and the dog huddling together on his couch in his sparse living room and bolted upstairs long enough to drag the blanket from his bed and take it back down to them. "You want something hot to drink?" His coat was still draped around her shoulders as he spread the blanket across them.

Abby shook her head. She'd dried her tears, but she was still clearly upset as she pulled the blue blanket up to her shoulders. "Don't you have to go in and make a report or something?"

He did. "Right now the two of you are my priority."

Her eyes went soft.

Dillon's hand emerged from the blanket and worked the fabric down until it was beneath his chin. "I can't breathe under there, Abby," he complained. A second later, Rex's nose popped out, too.

She laughed brokenly and pressed her cheek against the top of his head. "Sorry." She let out a shaking sigh. "Are you thirsty? Do you want something to drink?"

He shook his head. His gaze seemed to be glued to Sloan. "Told you he was a White Hat," he whispered to Abby, though Sloan could hear him well enough.

"I know, sweetie." Abby's eyes met Sloan's, and the trust in them was strong enough to shake him. "He's even more of one than you know."

Sloan tugged at his collar and was vaguely surprised to remember that he was still in his dress uniform. He yanked his tie loose, but it didn't seem to ease the vise tightening around his throat. "I'm going to go change."

Abby nodded. She closed her eyes and leaned her head back on the couch as if all she wanted to do was sleep, even though it was barely past six o'clock.

He headed for the stairs again but veered off for the front door when he heard someone knocking.

Both Dee Crowder *and* Tara were standing on the porch, looking equally wild-eyed. "I was at the bank when I heard," Tara said. "Are you all right?" Her gaze raced over him as if she were looking for proof otherwise.

"*I'm* fine."

"Some nice timing you have, Deputy," Dee said, moving past them to cross the room toward Abby. She sat on the couch next to her friend and put her arm around her shoulders.

Sloan exhaled, knowing whatever time he was going to have alone with Abby and Dillon had just ended. It would take an explosion to unseat either Tara or Dee now. He squeezed his sister's shoulder. "Will you stay here with them while I go over to the sheriff's office?"

She nodded immediately. "Should I call Axel?"

He shook his head. "No need. Max isn't going to let Bobby go anywhere. Everyone's safe."

"Thanks to you, from what I've been hearing."

"You didn't see Abby," he murmured. "She would have taken the guy's head off with the fireplace poker if I hadn't gotten there when I did." He didn't wait around to hear what his sister had to say about that. He just grabbed his keys and left to take care of business as rapidly as he could.

Rapidly, though, turned out to be a relative term, and it was several hours later before he was able to return. When he pulled up in his driveway, light was spilling from the front windows of his house, and something tightened inside his chest.

He ignored the feeling and went inside, immediately spotting Dillon where he was sprawled sleeping on the couch. The blanket from Sloan's bed was gone, but the kid was covered by Sloan's jacket, and Rex was on top of that. The dog opened his eyes and watched Sloan. But Rex didn't budge, and Sloan rubbed the dog's head as he studied Dillon.

He wondered if Calvin and his mother were sleeping just as soundly, knowing they were safe from Bobby for at least a little while.

He could hear the soft voices from the kitchen, and he gave Rex a final pat before moving silently in that direction. The three women were sitting around his kitchen table, but as soon as they heard him, they looked up. Dee was the first one to hop to her feet. "Gotta go!" She scurried past Sloan, giving him a wink.

His sister was almost as quick. "Dinner's at Jefferson and Emily's this Sunday," she told him. They were Axel's parents. "Do I need to twist your arm?"

He gave her a resigned look, though he was more interested in looking at Abby. She had dark circles under her eyes and had his blanket wrapped around her like a shawl. "We'll be there," he told his sister.

She blinked once, obviously noticing the *we* part. "Well, hallelujah," she murmured as she reached up to kiss his cheek. "Get some sleep, Abby," she ordered softly before hurrying out also.

A few seconds later, they heard the distinct click of the front door closing.

"And then there were two," he said quietly.

Her eyes searched his. "What happened?"

"Max is sitting on him. There won't be a judge available for an arraignment until Monday morning. He's got him until then, at the earliest."

"I'm going to need to make a statement."

He nodded once, not surprised that she'd reached the conclusion on her own. "You've got all weekend," he assured her. "You won't have to see Bobby—"

"I'd *like* to see him sitting in a jail cell," she interrupted, sounding fierce. "Preferably in shackles and chains."

"I should have gotten there sooner."

Her brows pulled together. "Why? You had no more reason to expect him to show up at my house than I did."

"I knew about the report you'd made about Calvin. I should have suspected."

She slowly pushed the blanket off her shoulders. She was still wearing only her robe. "Everyone in town probably knew about that report as soon as I made it."

"It's supposed to be confidential. If I find out Pam had anything to do with the news getting out, I'm going to—" He broke off when Abby reached out and pressed her fingers to his lips.

"Stop," she whispered. "This is nobody's fault but Bobby's. He's the one who abused his family. He's the one who invaded my house. How anybody finds out anything in this town doesn't matter. What matters is that he's been stopped."

"We should've been able to stop him before this." He pinched the bridge of his nose and turned to pace the kitchen. "Family protective services has been at that house more times than I want to think about. I should have seen that he'd started in on Calvin, too."

Abby hated hearing the blame in Sloan's voice that he directed squarely at himself. She walked up behind him and slid her hands over his tight shoulders, feeling the flinch he gave.

But he didn't move away, and she squeezed her fingers, kneading his back. "Bobby's the Black Hat here."

Sloan turned, his eyebrow lifting, and she realized she'd used Dillon's terminology. "You know what I mean. Bobby's the bad guy. Period." It seemed strange standing there with her hands digging into his shoulders while he faced her, and she slowly lowered her hands. "Do you know what's happened with Calvin?"

"Family protective services has him placed in a foster home for now."

"He wasn't at school yesterday or today."

"Not surprised."

"What about his mother?"

"They have to determine if she was part of the problem or a victim."

She thought of that poor, fearful woman she'd met on the sidewalk outside of Ruby's. "Victim."

"I think so, too, but Lorraine's got a terminal case of stand-by-her-man. I hope she'll choose to stand by her son this time." His lips twisted and he ran his hands down her arms with a frightening sense of finality. "You're beat." He stepped around her and moved toward the loaf of bread that was sitting out on the table. "Were you able to eat something?"

Feeling a little chilled, Abby nodded. "I can make you a sandwich."

"You don't have to make me anything." He twisted his head around as if his neck ached. "You can take my bed," he said abruptly.

It had been difficult not to poke around upstairs while he'd been gone, but she'd resisted the urge. If Tara hadn't been there, Abby wasn't sure if she'd have been able to keep Dee from egging her right into it. So she didn't know what sort of room or bed situation he had going on up there. "What about you?"

He shrugged. "I'll make do."

She chewed the inside of her lip. She truly had no desire to go next door to her own place, though she knew they'd have to soon enough. "There's no reason not to go back home. I'm being a ninny," she admitted. "But I don't want to go back in there unless it's during the cold light of day."

"You're not a ninny," he dismissed, sounding gruff. "You were going to bean the guy with an iron poker if you had to."

She swallowed, shuddering. It was still too vivid. All

she had to do was close her eyes and she could feel Bobby looming over her and looking crazed.

She heard Sloan curse. Then he slid his arm around her and pulled her against his chest. She couldn't keep herself from clinging to him. From pressing her ear against his chest where she could hear his steady heartbeat. Feel his steady breathing.

"I wanted to kill him," she whispered. "I never thought I'd feel such—" She broke off, not even able to articulate what she'd felt. "He hurt his own son. Scared Dillon out of his mind. God only knows what sort of nightmares he'll have now."

"Why does he have them in the first place?"

Sloan's hands slowly moved up and down her spine. He had never taken the time to change out of his uniform, and the fabric of his shirt felt smooth and crisp against her cheek. And beneath that, he was warm. Steady. Safe.

"His mother used to leave him alone for hours on end."

"You never refer to her as your mother, too."

She pulled back enough to look up at him. "It's hard to think of her as mine, though biologically she is. I have no relationship with her and don't want one." She thought about it for a moment. "It probably sounds shocking, but I really don't have any feelings toward her at all except for disgust at the way she cared for Dillon. The parents who counted for *me* were Minerva and Thomas Marcum."

He didn't look shocked, though. "And the parent who'll count for Dillon will be Abby." He said it as if it were already fact. Then he set her away from him and moved, looking suddenly restless. "Were her parental rights severed? Is it official?"

She tried not to think he'd put the granite-topped island between them as a barrier, even though it seemed that way. "I'm legally Dillon's guardian. I don't expect her to ever come back wanting him. She never did with me. But if she did, she wouldn't get anywhere. I have the assurance of several family-court judges on that particular score. Dillon's not going anywhere."

He studied her. His jaw was roughened by a dark shadow but not enough to mask its sharp angles. "You scare the hell out of me," he said abruptly.

Her stomach hollowed. "Why?"

He rubbed his hand down his face. Clawed his fingers through his hair. "You're twenty-three freaking years old."

"You want me to lie?" She smiled weakly. "Pad my age with a few years?" She pressed her palm against the cool granite, letting it steady her. "Shouldn't it matter less about the years and more about the life? There's ten years between us, not fifty."

"Might as well be," he muttered. His gaze drilled into hers. "You felt like you wanted to kill Bobby. Well, I *have* killed."

She swallowed hard. "Because you were doing your job?"

"While I was a Deuce."

"While you *rode* with the Deuces."

His lips twisted. "Don't romanticize it, Abby. I spent nearly a year closed up in a federal penitentiary just so my cover held water before I even got close to the Deuces, much less became one of them. There were whole years when there was no difference between them and me."

"Sloan." She spread her hands. "Of course there was a difference. If there hadn't been, you wouldn't be here now! You would have stayed with them. They'd have never known the truth. None of them would have seen the inside of a jail cell because of the evidence *you* brought to light."

His lips tightened. "The only reason I finished the job was because of Maria. She was a cocktail waitress where we'd hang." He went silent. The only sound came from the faint tick of the clock on the stove.

She pressed her tongue hard against the roof of her mouth, aching from the way he said her name. *Maria.*

"We got involved," he finally said. "And she hated thinking she'd fallen for a Deuce. She hated everything about them, but she couldn't get away from 'em because she already knew more about them than she should." He yanked off his loosened tie as if it were strangling him and balled it up in his fist.

"You loved her," Abby concluded softly. "So you told her the truth."

"And I got her killed because of it."

Her eyes burned. "I'm sorry."

"So am I." He turned on his heel and left the kitchen.

Abby's breath slowly eked out of her. She listened to the clock tick. Listened to the silence.

She could gather up Dillon and take him home. There was no bogeyman there. He was safely locked up in a jail cell for now. She could give Sloan space.

She ran her hand over the cool granite and heard a soft sound from above her. He'd gone upstairs.

She gathered up the blanket he'd given her—the one that smelled like him that she'd stayed huddled in for the past several hours—and balled it up in her arms, pressing her face into its softness for a moment.

Then she left the kitchen and padded silently past Dillon. He was still sleeping on the couch. Even Rex was snoring softly.

She reached the foot of the stairs and put her hand on the wooden newel-post. There wasn't much light coming from up there, but there was enough.

She put her foot on the first step and very nearly lost her nerve and turned around. But she didn't. She climbed the second step. And the third. And each one after that just got easier. At the top, she turned in the direction of the light and found Sloan sitting on the foot of a wide bed. It had no blanket. Only rumpled white sheets.

He was still in his uniform. His tie still balled in his fist.

She set the blanket on the bed and silently tugged the tie free from his hands. He didn't fight her. But she felt his gaze burning between her shoulder blades when she turned and smoothed out the tie carefully on the top of the chest of drawers across from the bed.

Then she turned back and crouched at his feet and began undoing the laces of his highly polished shoes. When they were loose enough, she pulled them off his feet then rolled off his socks and set them neatly aside.

Now the only thing she could hear was the sound of her own pulse clanging inside her head.

But she was here. And he hadn't told her to go.

She pushed to her feet and took his hands, pulling him up.

His eyes narrowed, but he stood, and she led him around to the side of the bed. She unbuttoned his shirt and tugged it off his shoulders. The white T-shirt beneath clung to his muscular shoulders, but that wasn't what made her breath catch in her throat. Nor was it the tattoo spreading below the short sleeve of his undershirt. It was the ugly scar tissue rippling over his right biceps. Maybe there'd come a time to ask about it.

But not now.

Reminding herself that she was a trained nurse didn't keep her hands from trembling as she undid his leather belt. It slithered from the belt loops when she tugged it free of his pants. She coiled it up and set it on the felt-lined tray sitting on top of the chest.

Nothing about Sloan moved except his eyes, which followed her as she came back and stood in front of him. She undid his pants, tugged them down his hips and willed herself not to pay too much attention to the dark gray boxer briefs he wore beneath as she kneeled and waited for him to step out of his trousers. Once he had, she shook them out and folded them over the back of the straight-backed chair in the corner.

She returned to stand in front of him once again. She started to lightly touch his shoulders, but she curled her fingers into her fists and reached around him instead to pull back the top sheet and smooth out the bunched-up pillows. The bed was as neat as she could make it in just those few seconds, and she looked at him. "Lie down," she said quietly.

His gaze flickered. The mattress sank a little when he sat down on the side of it. She waited, and after a moment, he let out a sigh and stretched out on his side, facing her.

She smoothed the sheet over him then turned off the lamp that was sitting on the nightstand next to him, plunging the room into darkness.

"Where are you going?" His voice was deep. A man's. But the question behind it could have come from her little brother.

"Nowhere," she soothed calmly. She walked around the bed, and her hand found the blanket where she'd left it. Then she climbed onto the mattress and stretched out behind him, spreading the blanket over them both. It was strange—her heart was pounding heavily, but she'd never felt more calm. She slid her arm over him, and her palm found the center of his chest. She pressed her cheek against the soft cotton knit stretched over his tense back. "Go to sleep, Sloan," she whispered. "I'm not going anywhere."

She didn't close her eyes. She didn't sleep. She simply

counted her heartbeats. Breathed slowly, knowing that he would feel the movement against him.

And a long, long while later, she felt a deep breath shudder through him, and he closed his hand tightly around hers.

Only then did she close her eyes.

Only then did she sleep.

Dawn was a silvery glow outside the slanted blinds at the window when Abby next opened her eyes. Sometime during the night, Sloan and she had turned over, and their positions had reversed. His arm was a heavy weight clamped over her waist.

She lay there for a long while, listening to his steady breathing; it wasn't quite a snore but obviously he was sleeping soundly. And while the idea of happily lying there with him for the rest of her days was lovely in theory, it wasn't exactly practical. Moving gingerly, she managed to slide out from beneath his arm without seeming to disturb his sleep and scooted off the foot of the bed. She glanced out the window as she passed it and realized it looked down on the side of her house and her own bedroom window.

Had he ever looked out, thinking of her?

She quickly turned away and silently slipped downstairs, where she visited the powder room tucked next to a room that could have been an office or a bedroom if it had possessed even one stick of furniture. She cracked the back door open long enough to let out Rex. For once, he cooperated beautifully, and in seconds he trotted back inside, where he immediately returned to the living room and hopped onto the couch near Dillon's feet. He circled a few times then settled in a ball and lowered his head on Dillon's leg. Her brother didn't even stir.

She adjusted the coat still draped over him like a blanket, and when he slept on, as peacefully as she'd ever seen him, she tightened the tie on her robe again and crept back up the stairs to Sloan's bedroom.

He hadn't moved, either, so she carefully worked her way back to where she'd been when she'd wakened, right down to the wonderful detail of his arm lying heavily across her waist.

She let out a long breath and closed her eyes.

Then Sloan's lax fingers tightened. They moved and spread and pressed flat against her belly, pulling her entire backside from shoulders on down solidly against him. "Wondered if you'd come back." His voice sounded rusty with sleep but that was the *only* thing that was sleeping where he was concerned.

That fact was glaringly noticeable, and the heat that collected deep inside her was instantaneous. She tried to speak, but only a garbled sound came out.

His knee crooked against the back of hers, and his hand ran possessively from her belly up over her hip. She could feel the heat of his palm even through her robe.

"Also been wondering what you had on underneath this thing." His fingers inched along the flannel, slowly drawing it up her leg. "If anything."

She let out a careful breath, thinking about the pretty panties she could have purchased at Tara's shop. If she hadn't chickened out, she wouldn't now be wearing her plain white cotton. "Nothing exciting."

"I don't know about that," he murmured. His palm slid beneath the flannel and curved over her upper thigh then slid behind it, gliding up over her hip, back down then up again. Gaining another inch with each pass, and making it increasingly difficult for her to remain still.

When he reached the narrow edge of her panties and

slid his fingers beneath, her lips parted and she hauled in a soundless breath.

His hand palmed her rear then tormentingly inched between her legs, where there was no mistaking her arousal. "That's pretty exciting," he murmured.

She moaned, shifting restlessly and much too quickly as his hand moved again but only to unknot her tie belt and draw the flannel away from her body. He kissed the shoulder he bared. "That's pretty exciting, too."

He shifted, his thigh sliding over hers and nudging her onto her back. His eyes roved over her as he slowly spread the robe, leaving her wearing nothing at all but her panties. "Ex." His fingers grazed oh-so-quickly over the juncture between her thighs again then trailed up the flat of her belly. "Cite." His fingertip circled one rigid nipple, then the other, then dragged over the hollow at the base of her throat, up her neck and stopped beneath her chin. He tilted it upward, toward his lips. "Ting," he whispered and kissed her softly.

And all the while he kissed her, his palm slid back down again, retracing its path. Lingering longer. Not teasing, but promising. When his hand glided over the center of her, she gasped. Then his fingers moved, swirled, and she shuddered, rocking needfully against him.

His breathing roughened. "Exciting, all right." He kissed her harder, only to pull back. His hands deliberately gentled. Slowed. His kiss turned sweet.

Her heart felt as if it were cracking open. She loved him. She knew she did. But his tenderness was almost more than she could bear, because she didn't know how she was going to survive it when he left.

And leave, he would.

"Don't stop now," she managed to say, pretending that her throat wasn't tightening and her heart wasn't breaking. She dragged at his T-shirt. "Wouldn't want to be rude, would you?"

He smiled a little. He pulled back enough to yank the shirt off, revealing the tattoo in its entirety. She caught her breath. The complicated design spread over his entire left shoulder and fanned out over his pec. "It must have taken days," she whispered. *"Why?"*

"Part of the job."

His hand slid along her cheek. "You want me to put my shirt back on?"

His thumb brushed over her lips, and she had to close her eyes against the tears that wanted to come. "No." She ran her hand deliberately over the tattoo. It was just ink. *He* was smooth and warm.

"If you want me to stop," he murmured, "just tell me. Something you don't like, you say so."

She let out a strangled laugh. Her body was humming, desperate for more, while he was only concerned that he might hurt her.

He would, too. She knew it. But it wasn't the hurt beyond his bed that counted here.

She rubbed her finger against the line between his brows. "I don't think that's going to happen." She shoved at his shoulders and pushed him flat on his back. She kicked off her panties and straddled him then leaned over until her breasts were flattened against the hard planes of his chest. Sensations buffeted her at every turn. Physically, there was nothing about him that wasn't hard. Honed. But inside, she knew he was even more vulnerable than she.

"I'm not going to break, Sloan." She kissed his bristly chin. Tugged gently at his lower lip with her teeth. "Please don't treat me like I will."

His hands closed over her rear, pulling her down against

him, and she gasped at the thrilling feel of him pulsing against her. His eyes searched hers. "Are you sure?"

She rocked her hips slowly, and her eyes nearly rolled back in her head with pleasure. "Never more."

His hand left her only long enough to reach for the drawer in the nightstand. He pulled out a foil packet. "You *that* sure?"

She took it from him and tore it open. "Still questioning?"

He gave a strangled groan. "You're killing me here, Abby."

She leaned over again, her lips hovering above his. "I'm a nurse, remember?" She felt the quick twitch of his lips, and it made her feel braver. "Show me, Sloan," she whispered. "Let me make it better."

His hands clamped on her head, and he kissed her deeply. Then he showed her. And when his fingers fisted around the bedding beside him rather than her, she tugged at his hands until he let go and guided them to her hips instead and slowly took him in.

"I don't want to hurt you," he gritted.

"You aren't," she promised, lying only a little. The pressure was immense, but he was inside her and she loved him, and soon the pressure was just pleasure that kept growing. And when she didn't think she could feel anything more, he groaned her name—*her* name—and he turned, tucking her beneath him. His palms slid against hers as he lifted their linked hands above her head, and he drove even harder, even deeper, and the bed squeaked softly.

Even though she'd promised herself that she wouldn't cry, helpless tears leaked from the corners of her eyes, because there were only so many ways her emotions could escape. And then his hands left hers and cradled her face.

"Look at me." His voice was low. Rough. "Abby. Look at me."

Everything inside her was tightening. Opening her eyes felt nearly impossible. But she dragged them open.

His face was tense, his jaw tight. But it was the tenderness in his eyes as he stared into hers that made it feel as if her soul were cracking wide. "It's okay," he whispered. "Let yourself go, sweetheart. I've got you."

He reached down, one hand clamping around her hip, tilting her, and she felt him even deeper. As if the blood pulsing inside him were her blood; as if her heartbeat had become his. Then there was no more except the ecstasy of exploding with him in a perfect shower of light.

Chapter Fourteen

"Abby! Can we have oatmeal for breakfast?" The sound of Dillon's voice was accompanied by the pounding of his footsteps on the stairs, waking Sloan. Abby, too, he noticed regretfully when her warm body shifted away.

"My brother," she whispered urgently.

Sloan's brain suddenly snapped into gear. Half the morning was already spent, he realized, as he bolted from the bed through the doorway of his bathroom. He shut the door just as Abby was yanking on her robe and shoving her tumbled hair out of her face.

"Good morning, Mr. Marcum," he heard her calmly say a moment later. "And, yes, I imagine we can have oatmeal. Why don't we go downstairs and see whether Sloan has any, or if we need to get it from our house?"

Sloan stared at himself in the mirror as he listened to their fading voices as they went downstairs.

Abby was calm, but his heart was thundering as though

he'd just escaped being caught committing the worst of crimes.

He'd never really subscribed to the notion that a man stole a willing woman's virginity. He also knew that he'd never taken a woman to bed who'd had less experience than he. And *his* first time, his partner had possessed considerably more.

But with Abby?

He rubbed his chest as if her fingers were still pressed against it.

He didn't know what the hell he was feeling, but he knew it wasn't familiar.

He looked at his reflection. For once, his eyes weren't bloodshot. Guess that was what happened when he actually slept the entire night through.

No nightmares. No insomnia.

Abby had put her arms around him and he'd slept like a damned baby. Last time he could remember sleeping so soundly, he'd been a kid.

He turned on the shower and tried not to wish too hard that Abby was there with him. Oatmeal was a good way to start the day. But making love with her was a helluva lot better. He'd already discovered that.

Twice.

Then he realized he was grinning like a damn fool and he didn't care.

Laughing at himself, he stepped into the water. The sooner he showered, the sooner he could go downstairs and join them.

"Is Sloan your boyfriend *now?*"

Abby hesitated only briefly before setting the empty cereal bowl she'd found in Sloan's cupboards on the table for Dillon. "No," she said calmly. She was excruciatingly aware of the sound of the shower from upstairs. "Why?"

Dillon wrinkled his face, studying her as if she was dim. "'Cause he rescued you and everything." *Duh.*

"You did some rescuing yourself," she reminded him. "I told you to stay locked in your room. I think maybe I should get after you for not doing exactly what I said and climbing out your window instead."

"It was a 'mergency," he pointed out. There was no panic in his eyes. He was simply stating a fact.

She smiled and reached across to tweak his nose. "Yes. It was an emergency. And you were very brave to get out that way and go for help."

Rex suddenly left his spot at Dillon's feet to run across the kitchen, his paws sliding on the smooth travertine. She turned to see Sloan.

His wet hair was slicked back, nearly black. He'd shaved and was wearing faded jeans that hung enticingly on his hips, with an equally faded blue waffle-weave shirt. His feet were bare, and the lines radiating from his dark eyes were crinkling with a smile.

Looking at him made her blood hum. But seeing that smile made her tremble with hope. She might as well have been Rex, pretty much shaking with delight.

She quickly turned to busy herself with the oatmeal on the stove and nearly shrieked when she felt Sloan slide his arm around her from the back and kiss her on the neck.

"G'morning," he murmured. His fingers slid wickedly inside the lapel of her robe where Dillon couldn't see and toyed with her breast. "Looks like it's getting hot."

She swatted at his forearm. He grinned, looking amused, and tucked her robe back in place before moving away. He leaned over to scratch Rex behind the ears, and the dog groaned with delight. "Dill, you want to go out on the motorcycle again?"

Abby stared into the oatmeal she was stirring. She felt as if she'd fallen down the rabbit hole or something. Everything appeared so...normal.

Yet it wasn't.

"Abby says you're not her boyfriend," Dillon informed Sloan, instead of answering.

She looked over her shoulder at her brother, giving him a warning stare. But he was focused singly on Sloan.

"But *I* think you are," he finished.

Sloan angled the chair opposite her brother and sat. He stretched out his long legs. Leisurely. As if this sort of thing were an everyday occurrence for him. "Does that idea bother you?"

"Only if you make her sad," Dillon replied immediately, as if he'd put quite a bit of thought into it.

"Well," Sloan answered seriously, "I'd better try really hard not to do that, then."

She realized she was gaping and turned back to the oatmeal. It was bubbling and spitting, and she quickly turned off the gas flame beneath it. She poured the hot cereal into two bowls and nearly tossed them onto the table in front of Sloan and her brother. Dillon made a face, holding up the empty bowl she'd already given him, and flushing a little, she returned it to the cupboard. "I don't know what you have to put on top of the oatmeal," she said vaguely, already turning to escape. "I'm going home. It's time I got dressed." She knew her little brother would be perfectly happy to stay there with Sloan and eat.

"Geez," she heard Dillon say as she practically skidded out of the room with about as much grace as Rex. "What's with her?"

She didn't wait around to overhear whatever Sloan

might answer. She just pushed her feet into her snow boots and fled.

She was halfway across the yard between their houses when she realized she had put her boots on the wrong feet, but she plowed on and hurried through her front door.

It had been left unlocked all night, and it wasn't until she made it to the relative sanctity of her own bedroom that she realized she hadn't given Bobby Pierce's threatening attack a single thought on her way over.

She let out a disbelieving laugh and scrubbed her hands down her face. She retrieved clean clothes—trying not to dwell on the fact that she'd left her panties buried somewhere among Sloan's bedsheets—and took the first cold shower she'd ever willingly taken in her life.

When she came out a while later, scrubbed and wearing goose bumps beneath her turtleneck and jeans, she stopped short at the sight of Sloan leaning against her breakfast counter. "Where's Dillon?"

"Outside talking to Gilcrest." His eyes roved over her. "You okay?"

Besides having mush for knees? She realized she was chewing the inside of her cheek and made herself stop. "Fine. You?"

The creases deepened at the corner of his lips. "Fine." His voice was mild. "When do you want to make your statement?"

"Does Dillon have to be there?"

"I don't think that'll be necessary."

"So he can stay here with you while I go and take care of it now?"

His eyes narrowed thoughtfully. "You don't need me to go with you?"

Yes! She focused on pulling on her boots, correctly this time. "It's just as well if I do it on my own."

"Why?"

She straightened and tightened the clip that she'd used to pin up her hair. "Because if I get used to depending on you, it's just going to be harder when you leave."

He studied her for a moment. "I'm here now."

As much as it stung, she appreciated his not pretending that he was going to be around for the long haul. She yanked open the coat closet and pulled out a short white jacket and a yellow scarf.

"Maybe *I* need to go with you," he added.

She looked at him. "Officially? Or because you're feeling weird about what happened?"

"Making love with you wasn't weird," he answered. "Don't look so serious, Abby. That's usually my job." He nudged her chin, tilting it up with his knuckle. "One of the first things I noticed when we met was that you had a face made for smiling."

"You're just saying that."

He held up his hand as if he were taking an oath. "Nope."

He made it too easy to like him. It ought to have made things easier. But it didn't. "Someone is going to have to watch Dillon, and as nice as Mr. Gilcrest is, he's ninety. I'd feel bad even asking him."

"What about Dee?"

She looked past him to see the clock in the kitchen. "She's probably on her way to pole dancing about now."

He grunted. "I'd be shocked, except I know that's the exercise class Pam Rasmussen's always going on about. I'll call my sister. She works at the shop on Saturday mornings, and it's just down the street from the sheriff's office."

"I don't want to put her out." She also didn't want Tara reading more into things between Sloan and Abby than she already did.

"She'll be pissed if she finds out I didn't ask her. Of course, you don't have to make your statement right this minute, either."

She shook her head. "I want to get it done." Before she could second-guess her decision, she went to the door and called to Dillon. He came running, and she waved at Mr. Gilcrest before shutting the door. "Go put on some clean clothes," she told Dillon.

"Are we going to see Grandma?"

"Sure," she decided suddenly. Visiting her would be a good way to remove the bad taste of having to officially recount Bobby's actions. "But first there's some business I have to take care of. So be quick."

Sloan called his sister while Dillon trotted down the hall toward his bedroom. A few minutes later, they were headed out the door. They dropped Dillon off at Classic Charms, where Tara greeted him with a wide smile and a cowboy hat that she plunked on his head. "Want to help me unpack some boxes?"

He nodded and didn't give Abby so much as a second glance.

"I think my brother is infatuated with your sister," she told Sloan as they crossed the street toward his office.

"Nah. He's got it bad for Chloe."

Abby shook her head. "Please. She trounced him at 'White Hats.'"

He reached past her to open the front door of his office. "Never underestimate the appeal of a woman who gives just as good as she gets." Then he lifted his hand, greeting the man sitting at the dispatcher's desk. "Max around?"

"I'm here." The sheriff's voice came from an office behind the cluster of desks arranged in an open area, and a moment later the tall man appeared in the doorway. He smiled and beckoned to Abby when he saw her. "Come on in."

She hadn't thought she'd be nervous. But she suddenly was.

Sloan seemed to realize it. He wrapped his hand around hers. "It's going to be okay."

She knew he was talking about the task ahead of her. But just then it felt as if he meant so much more. "Okay."

He squeezed her hand. His eyes crinkled with a smile. "Thatta girl."

While the frightening incident with Bobby Pierce had been mercifully brief thanks to Sloan's timely arrival, Abby quickly realized that making an official complaint about the entire thing was not, and by the time she finally signed her name at the bottom of the statement, several hours had passed. She felt as if every speck of energy had been wrung out of her.

"I know this wasn't pleasant," the sheriff said, looking kind. "But the better we're prepared with the charges for the judge, the longer Bobby is going to be out of everyone's life."

"He needs to be out of his son's life."

"I agree. And we're taking care of that as well, thanks to you." He took the papers she'd signed and set them on the credenza behind his desk. "In the meantime, if you want to speak with someone, a victim's advocate—"

She shook her head. "I'm good."

"Okay. But the offer stays open."

"So are we done?" She pushed to her feet. "My brother is probably driving Sloan's sister up the wall by now."

"We're done." He stood up and accompanied her through the doorway. Sloan was sitting at his desk but rose as soon as he saw them. "She's all yours, Deputy."

The sheriff had no way of knowing how badly Abby wished that she *were* all Sloan's. "Thank you, Sheriff."

"Max'll do." He smiled and returned to his office.

Sloan handed over her coat. "Doing okay?" His eyes roved over her as if he were looking for evidence that she wasn't.

She took the clip out of her hair and rubbed her fingers through it. "Pooped, actually." He'd been with her for the first hour before leaving her alone with the sheriff.

"You did great."

"Maybe. But Dillon's going to be disappointed when I tell him I just don't have the energy to drive to Braden this afternoon." The sun was bright in the sky when they left the office, and she squinted, looking across the street toward Tara's shop.

"I'll drive you if you still want to go," he offered.

"You'd do that?"

He laughed softly. "It's not exactly the moon, sweetheart. It's just Braden."

But to her, it wasn't "just" anything.

He was here now. He'd said it. And she wanted every bit of "now" with him that he was willing to give. So she nodded.

They collected Dillon. He chattered throughout the entire drive to Braden, pointing out the school that he'd gone to and their old house. Even though it was the middle of winter, there was a new tire swing hanging from the tree in the backyard, and Abby felt good knowing that the home where she'd grown up would still have children in it.

When they arrived at Braden Bridge, they found Minerva in the sunroom, fussing over the potted plants that she loved. Her hair was silver and her face was lined, but she had a beaming smile. The only thing missing was a spark of recognition in her gray eyes as she greeted them. She didn't seem shocked when Abby kissed her cheek or take much notice when she introduced Sloan. But Minerva sat right down and pulled Dillon on her lap, listening with appropriate awe as he told her how he'd climbed out the window to call for help when Abby needed it, and that right there made the visit worthwhile.

But she also knew they couldn't stay for too long. It was better to end their visit earlier than she wanted than to tire Minerva too greatly and cause her the distress that always followed. So they soon walked her back to her small suite, where Abby helped her grandmother settle into her favorite chair.

"Your young man reminds me of Thomas," Minerva whispered. "The way he looks you right in the eye when he speaks." She nodded. "A good choice." She picked up the framed photograph of Abby's grandfather from the little table beside her chair and showed it to Abby as if she'd never seen it before. "It was a whirlwind that lasted fifty years." Her narrow fingers brushed tenderly over the picture, and her gaze found Sloan. "He fell in love with my chocolate cookies, you see. We married a month to the day after that."

If Abby hadn't already fallen in love with Sloan, she would have now just from the way he smiled so gently at her grandmother. "I can understand why," he told her. "I believe I've had your chocolate cookies, too."

Minerva smiled again, but even as she did, Abby knew the moment had passed. She recognized the faraway expression, the suddenly restless movements of her hands, and knew that it was time to leave. She returned the picture frame to the table and brushed a kiss against her grandmother's soft cheek. "We'll come back soon to visit."

Minerva nodded politely. "Tell your grandfather that he's watering the begonias too much," she told Dillon.

Her brother nodded. "I will, Grandma."

As soon as they left the room, Abby quickly excused herself and hurried down the hall to the ladies' room.

"She's gonna go in there and cry," Dillon told Sloan. "But you can't go in there," he added when Sloan took a step toward the door. "I think it's against the law."

He almost smiled. "Not exactly." He hated thinking she was in there alone. He wasn't blind. Even though she'd had a calm smile on her face as they'd visited her grandmother, he'd seen the strain behind it. "She do that every time you visit?"

"Uh-huh." Dillon hopped from one floor tile to another. "She'll be okay, though."

"How do you know?"

"Because she told me sometimes a person needs t' cry. And she feels better after she gets it all out. Can I ride on your motorcycle when we get home?"

It would be dark by the time they got back to Weaver. Sloan figured Abby would be even less thrilled with the notion. "Tomorrow," he promised. "Maybe you can talk your sister into having a ride, too."

"You can ask her." Dillon crouched then leaped to another tile. "All you gotta do is say *please*."

"Please," Sloan wheedled the next day.

He was sitting astride his big black motorcycle, holding out the helmet that Dillon had already surrendered after riding around the block a few times with Sloan.

"No, thank you," she said for the third time. She'd been sitting on the front porch step waiting for them to return and her butt was cold. Dillon was doing his level best to start another snowman since Frosty was little more than a headless hump at this point, but the snow was too dry to cooperate. "I don't like motorcycles."

Sloan's lips tilted. He set the helmet on the seat behind him and leaned his folded arms over the handlebars. "How do you know you won't like it if you've never tried it?"

She flushed all the way through. He'd said the same thing that morning when she'd awoken to his kisses on her thighs and he'd worked his way up with wicked intention. Of course, he'd been right. She'd nearly gone out of her mind from pleasure.

"Aren't we supposed to be leaving for your sister's Sunday dinner soon?"

"Don't know that it's Tara's dinner so much as the Clays in general," he drawled. "It's a thing with that whole family, and we've got over an hour, anyway. What are you afraid of, Abby? That you might like the feel of a Harley between your legs? It's not really walking on the wild side, you know." His eyes were amused and oh, so appealing. "Not unless thinking that way gets you going."

She covered her face, trying not to laugh. "I'm not leaving Dillon unattended, even to just ride around the block!" She pushed to her feet and dusted off the seat of her jeans with her mittens.

"Eh, leave him be," Mr. Gilcrest called from his front porch. "Boy's not going to go anywhere, and I ain't dead yet. He can sit and play checkers with me."

"Cool." Dillon abandoned his efforts to build a snowman appallingly quickly and started to run across the yard.

"Dillon! I didn't say you could go."

He slipped on the packed snow but managed not to fall. "Can I?"

Abby looked from his bright eyes to Sloan's. She wasn't at all certain that the two of them—three, if they'd roped in Mr. Gilcrest—hadn't somehow prearranged this.

"Oh, fine," she grumbled.

And she knew she'd really been had when Dillon bumped

his mitten-clad fist against Sloan's knuckles as he trotted past him.

Sloan held the helmet out to her. "You might like it."

"Don't count on it," she grumbled as she took the thing from him and pulled it over her head. It felt heavy and too large as she awkwardly swung her leg over the bike. Sloan told her where to keep her feet then pulled her hands around his waist.

She wondered what he'd do if she let her hand drift lower. He'd managed to shock the stuffing out of her that morning. Seemed as though a little turnaround was due.

He shifted his body, and the engine growled to life. Dillon was waving at her, and she managed to unclench her fingers long enough to wave back before the bike swayed in a curve and Sloan roared away from the house. She gasped, grabbing on to him again, and, though she couldn't be certain, she thought she felt his shoulders shaking with laughter.

Then they turned the corner at the end of the street, but he didn't head around the block like she expected. He headed away from town. And a few minutes later, he turned onto a narrow road that she'd never even been on and picked up speed.

Alarm shot through her. She leaned over his shoulder as much as she could, which wasn't much. "Where are we going?" she yelled.

His smile flashed. "Does it matter?"

Since she was wearing *his* helmet, that meant that he wasn't, and the wind was ruffling his thick hair. He looked more carefree than she'd ever seen him. The sky was blue, the land around them iced with snow. It was a beautiful winter afternoon, and he was smiling.

"No," she finally yelled.

He squeezed her hands where they were clenched together over his belly, and a moment later, the engine gained even more speed as they flew along the empty road.

The truth was, she'd go with him anywhere, as long as he asked.

Chapter Fifteen

By the time they returned nearly an hour later, Dillon and Mr. Gilcrest were still bundled up and sitting on the old man's porch, playing checkers.

Abby slid off the back of the motorcycle, feeling as exhilarated as she felt shaky. "I'm still vibrating inside," she admitted.

Sloan's eyebrow arched. "Intriguing."

She flushed. "It wasn't an invitation."

He laughed. "I'm going to put this back in the shed, and we can head out for dinner." He started the engine again and slowly steered the bike right across their snowy yards toward the back of his place.

"It was fun, huh," Dillon said when she retrieved him.

"Yes." She smiled up at Mr. Gilcrest. "Thanks for minding him."

He just waved his hand dismissively. "Boy plays a good game." Then he looked over his glasses at her. "If you want t' bring me some more of them cookies sometime, I guess that'd be all right."

She chuckled. "It's a deal."

"And tell that deputy of yours someone was snooping around his house lookin' for him."

Abby stiffened, her mind too quickly going to Bobby Pierce. But the man was safely in jail. "When?"

Mr. Gilcrest shrugged. "Thirty minutes ago or so. Drove one of them *government* cars." His tone made it plain what he thought of that. He pushed to his feet, looking stiff as he shuffled to his front door. "Keep an eye out for Marigold, will you? Damn cat's disappeared on me again."

"I will." She watched until he'd gotten safely inside then turned and hurried Dillon to their own house. While he cleaned up in the bathroom, she tended to Rex and changed into the new sweater that she hadn't yet worn. She brushed out her own hair, smoothed on some lip gloss and tried to pretend that going with Sloan to the Clays' family dinner wasn't a big deal even though it was.

"Abby." Sloan called her name, and she left her bedroom. When she came into the room, his eyes ran over her. "Dillon," he commented to her brother, "you've got yourself a pretty sister."

Dillon made a face as if he was gagging, but he giggled too much for it to have any effect.

"Thank you for that vote of confidence," Abby told him dryly. She retrieved her red coat and slid into it. "Someday you're going to need me to teach you how to drive so you can take a girl out on a date. And I'll remember how you just acted."

Dillon just giggled harder. "Sloan'll teach me how to drive, wontcha?"

Abby felt a pang. That was years down the road.

Sloan held back Rex even as he nudged Dillon out the door. "Sure thing, bud."

He saw the black sedan sitting in front of his house at the same moment that Abby did.

"Oh, right. Mr. Gilcrest mentioned…" She trailed off when she saw the way Sloan's jaw had whitened. She looked from him to the vehicle. A blond-haired man had gotten out. He was wearing a suit but no overcoat, and as he glanced around, his hand smoothed down his tie. "Do you know him?"

"I worked with him." His tone was flat. "On the Deuces case. Wait here."

He strode down the porch steps and crossed the lawn. "What the hell are you doing here, Sean?"

Abby closed her hands over Dillon's shoulders to keep him from following. She wanted to hear more of what they said, but Rex was barking inside the house, and Sloan had reached the other man near the car. Their voices were too low to make anything out.

Then the guy gave Sloan an envelope, and he looked back toward Abby.

She felt something clang shut inside her.

She could see it in his face. Read it in his posture.

Now had come to an end.

She couldn't even pound her fists and scream at the unfairness of it all. At the shortness of the time she'd been given.

"Dillon," she managed to say hoarsely. "Go back inside."

"But—"

"Go!" She winced when his face fell, and she touched his cheek. Swallowed. Rex could hear them and was nearly howling. She wished she could. "Please. I'll be there in a little bit."

His smooth brow crumpled, but he went back inside. Through the door, howls immediately became yips of joy.

At least someone was happy.

The black sedan was driving away, and she watched Sloan walk toward her. He stopped next to what was left of poor Deputy Frosty.

"They want you back," she said.

She'd expected it, but it still felt as if she'd been kicked in the stomach.

Sloan hated the look on Abby's face. A look he was responsible for. He wasn't any different than Bobby Pierce; he just hadn't raised his fists to deliver the blow. He lifted the envelope. "Travel arrangements."

Her eyes went dark, but they were unflinching. "Chicago?"

He shook his head. "Florida." He rubbed his eyebrow and wanted to look away. But he didn't deserve a respite. "I leave tonight."

"What's in Florida?"

"Tony Diablo," he said. "Johnny was his cousin." He told her what Sean had said about the signs that the Deuces were reestablishing themselves.

"And they want you to stop him?"

"The agency fired me. Before." He saw the fresh shock in her eyes.

"You never said."

There were a lot of things he hadn't said. "I don't want to leave you, Abby." He took a step closer. "But—"

"But." Her lashes finally fell, hiding her gray eyes. "They want you back," she finished. "And you want to go."

"I want to know I ended things on *my* terms."

"Then you should go," she said huskily. "You should go get what you want."

He took a step closer and thought about the other time,

when he'd stood in her yard, and she'd clung to her porch rail. He could count the days that had passed since then, so how could so much have changed? "What do *you* want?"

Her lips twisted. He thought she wasn't going to answer. But that wasn't Abby's way.

Her lashes lifted. Her pretty gray eyes met his. "I want what my grandparents had." Her voice was husky. "I want fifty years with the man I love. I want forever." She squeezed the porch rail then let it go and turned to the door.

"Abby!"

Even through the red coat, he could see her shoulders stiffen. She didn't turn, but her head angled until he saw the fine line of her jaw.

"I…care—" God, it shouldn't be so hard to say the words "—*more* than care."

He saw her swipe her cheek. "I know you do." She still didn't look at him. "It's okay, Sloan. You don't have to worry about me. I've worn big-girl panties for a while now."

"Smart-i-tude."

She finally turned enough to look at him. Her eyes were wet. "Don't knock it," she said. "I always knew you would leave, Sloan. I just…just didn't think it would be this soon."

"I'm not leaving *you*."

Her lips twisted. "The result is the same."

Come with me. The words rang around inside his head like a gong reverberating. But come where? Tony Diablo was in Florida at the moment. There was no guarantee he'd stay there; it was highly likely that he wouldn't. Nothing was stable about where he was going; and everything about Abby shouted stability. Dillon needed it. Her grandmother needed it. Abby had moved to Weaver, but there was no way she'd put even more distance between her and where Minerva lived in Braden.

And he'd never put another woman he loved in danger because of his work.

"It's okay, Sloan," she said again, as if she knew exactly what was going on inside his head. Inside his heart. Hell. Maybe she knew better than he did.

She pushed open the door and stepped inside.

His foot lurched forward seemingly of its own accord. "Dillon—"

"It's better if I handle my brother," she said, looking protective.

Which just hurt that much more, knowing that Dillon needed protecting from *him*.

"I told you I was no hero."

"The only one who ever cared about that was you, Sloan. We just cared about *you*." She pushed open the door. "Be safe," she whispered.

And then she was gone, the door closing quietly, finally, behind her.

"Come on, Dillon," Abby coaxed. Just because their hearts were breaking didn't mean that it wasn't a Monday and that they didn't need to leave for school. "You've worked on that poster for weeks."

Since she'd told him that Sloan had to leave, Dillon had barely spoken a single word. The fact that he'd had a nightmare hadn't come as a surprise. His world had been shaken up.

But she'd gotten him through the rough patches before and she would again. At least with him to focus on, she wasn't falling apart completely herself.

But now he didn't want to enter the contest at all.

She brushed her fingers through his hair and kissed his forehead. "I know you'll miss Sloan, honey. But he'd want you to turn in your poster, too."

His lips twisted, but he grabbed the poster and carried it with him to the door.

She exhaled silently, and they left. She avoided looking at Sloan's house. The driveway was empty. It would stay that way.

One Monday morning down. Only a lifetime more to go.

She told Dee about him leaving when she popped her head in during her prep hour. "Well, that bastard!"

Abby shook her head, trying not to cry. "He's nothing of the sort."

Dee tossed up her hands and shook her head as if Abby were crazy. Maybe she was.

She didn't have to tell Mr. Gilcrest that he'd gone. When she took him over a fresh batch of cookies, he'd already known. "Saw for myself when he left with that suitcase of his," he'd said and patted her hand. "Boy'll be back."

Abby didn't have the heart to tell him that *he* was the crazy one, too.

January slid into February, and Principal Gage announced the winners of the contest from each grade. Dillon didn't win, and neither did Chloe, though he'd been convinced she would. February slid into March and March into April. Calvin Pierce finally returned to school now that his father had been transferred to a jail over in Gillette and was well out of reach. Calvin and his mother had left their house and were living in one of the apartments by Dee. Lorraine had started taking college courses online and was looking like a new woman. When she and Abby ran into each other outside of Ruby's one afternoon, Lorraine smiled shyly, and they shared a cup of coffee.

She continued playing spinster poker and took up the pole class on Saturdays, where Pam Rasmussen gossiped the whole while about everything from the rash of petty thefts the sheriff was certain were being perpetrated by teenagers, to the hot romance she was convinced her great uncle was secretly having, because there was no other explanation for his good humor of late.

Though she couldn't seem to stop looking at Sloan's house every time she walked by it, as if one day he'd miraculously be standing there, she did stop looking every day for the inevitable for-sale-or-rent sign to show up in the yard. And she stopped avoiding going to Classic Charms for fear of running into Tara. She learned more details about Sloan's life during the conversations she had with his sister than she ever had learned from him.

Life, as she had learned more than once, did move along whether she wanted it to or not.

May arrived, and she set out flowers for Mr. Gilcrest. She helped Dillon plant a little garden in the back of the house and surrounded it with wire so that Rex wouldn't dig in it. But he dug, anyway. And when she discovered a groundhog burrow that extended all the way to the woodpile behind Sloan's house, she understood why she couldn't keep Rex from clawing at the wood and barking at it every chance he got.

The school year ended, and Abby signed Dillon up for the same day camp that Chloe attended, and she took a part-time job at the hospital that would last until school began again in the fall. She even went out on a date with one of the doctors there. He was charming and fun. But he wasn't Sloan. She didn't go out with him again.

And one day, in the middle of June, she came home after her shift at the hospital and noticed the window in the front of his house was open.

Her heart climbed into her throat.

No sheriff's SUV in the driveway. No vehicle at all.

Just an open window. And it was much more likely one

of the break-ins that Pam talked about than Sloan suddenly returning.

She hadn't heard a single word from him since the day that black car had stopped in front of his house, and her life had lost its luster. Tara had promised to tell her if she ever heard that he was hurt. But not even Tara had heard from him.

Sloan had left Weaver and he hadn't looked back.

She ignored the open window and went into her own house. She changed out of her scrubs and pulled on denim shorts and a red tank top. She glanced out her bedroom window up at his bedroom window. Saw nothing but the closed blinds, the same way they'd been for months.

She whistled for Rex, and the dog trotted outside with her, obediently plopping his butt on the sidewalk as she walked down to stand in front of Sloan's house again and study that open window. She'd feel silly calling the sheriff because of it.

For all she knew, a Realtor had come by to look things over. It was a warm summer day. Why *not* open the window and let in some fresh air to a house that had been left, neglected and alone, for months?

"Come on, Rex." She headed back toward her house, but he suddenly bolted down the side yard, furiously barking the way he always did whenever he thought there was a chance of catching that groundhog. She followed. So far, she'd resisted Mr. Gilcrest's suggestion of shooting the rodent, but every time she went back to her garden and found he'd managed to get over or under the chicken wire she kept putting up, the more tempting the idea became.

Rex was going nearly crazy, barking with the ferocity of a canine who believed he was twice the size that he actually was, and she quickly realized it wasn't the groundhog that had him so agitated.

It was the fact that the door of Sloan's shed was ajar.

She grimaced and went a few steps closer. "I've already called the sheriff," she lied loudly. "And I've got my granddaddy's shotgun," she added for good measure. "I'm a mighty good shot, so you'd better think twice about what you're doing in there."

The old wood door creaked, and she hastily grabbed for Rex's collar and missed when he lunged for the opening.

"See you're still having trouble catching the dog," Sloan said as he scooped Rex out of midair. He pushed the shed door open the rest of the way with his shoulder, avoiding the dog's slathering tongue.

Abby could only stare.

His hair was shorter, the flecks of gray more apparent. They were echoed in the short moustache and goatee he wore. His T-shirt had a line drawing of a skull on the front, and his jeans hung on his hips. He was tan. Leaner. And he hadn't had any fat to spare before. The scar on his right biceps and the tattoo on his left seemed to fit right in.

He looked dangerous. He looked hard.

Except for his eyes.

She slowly straightened and wished she were wearing something a little more presentable than the cutoffs that she'd had since high school.

He angled his head and considered her. "If you're packing a shotgun, I'm not sure where you're hiding it, sweetheart. Those shorts are pretty short."

She crossed her arms. "What are you doing here?"

He set Rex down, much to the dog's disappointment. "I came to get something I wanted."

Pain rolled through her, so much sharper than it should have been after all this time. She could see behind him to his big black motorcycle. It took up nearly the entire space inside the shed. "I wondered when you'd make arrangements for the Harley." He hadn't taken it when he'd left. And nobody had come for it since.

He didn't even glance at the bike. "Your hair's longer."

She self-consciously touched her hair. Annoyed with herself, she dropped her hands. Pushed them in the back pockets of her shorts. "Yours isn't. Looking a lot grayer, too."

His lip tilted. "Missed that smart-i-tude. How's Dillon?"

"Good." She left it at that. If he wanted to know more, he was going to have to be specific. It had been five months since he'd said a word to her. She wasn't going to make the mistake of thinking he was there for any reason that had anything to do with her.

"Your grandmother?"

Her jaw tightened. "Her condition hasn't deteriorated."

"And you?" His eyes seemed to bore into hers. "Found anyone who has the next fifty years available?"

She turned on her heel and walked away.

"Abby, wait." He caught up to her and closed his hands around her arms, turning her to face him.

She couldn't look at him. It hurt too much. "I can't do this." She stepped back and his hands fell away. "Just take what you came for and go. Dillon's going to be here soon, and I don't want him seeing you. He's finally stopped asking when you'll be home."

He looked pained. "I know I hurt you. Both of you."

She wasn't going to deny what was so patently obvious.

"Are you…seeing anyone?"

"A resident from the hospital," she said without a shred of regret for exaggerating her one date.

"A doctor." Sloan's lips twisted. "Guess that stands to reason."

She smiled coolly. "He has a thing for girls in a nurse's cap. You? Anyone new you're tatting yourself up for?"

"Is it serious?"

"Terminally."

His jaw slanted. "Guess that's nothing more than I deserve. Probably giving him your grandmother's chocolate cookies."

"I bake a batch every week." He had no need to know they went to Mr. Gilcrest. She waved her hand at him. "You don't look like you're spending a lot of time wearing a suit and sitting behind a desk. What's the ATF have you doing? I guess the goatee is a little bit of a disguise, but—"

"I'm not with the ATF. Haven't been for four months."

She absorbed that. He hadn't raced back to Weaver, that was for sure. If she'd needed some sort of proof about the way he felt, that would seem to be it. She turned again to go.

"Not interested in what I *have* been doing?"

She stopped. Looked at him again. "Working on your tan by the looks of it."

His lips twisted. "I've been in the sun," he allowed. "Digging ditches, among other things."

"Why? Get yourself on a chain gang in preparation for something else undercover?"

"Getting my head clear," he said quietly. "Finally."

Her eyes suddenly prickled. "I'm glad for you," she managed to say.

"I'm sorry it took me so long."

Her chest ached. And standing there pretending was simply more than she could take. "You don't have to be sorry where I'm concerned."

"Right. Big-girl panties and all that."

She cleared her throat. "You should at least take a few minutes to see your sister."

"I will. I wanted to see you first."

"Why?"

"Because you're the reason I came home."

Home? She closed her eyes. "Sloan."

"I love you, Abby. I didn't want to. And I thought if I left, maybe it would go away. But every time I closed my eyes, you were there. Inside my head. Inside my heart."

She sank her teeth into her tongue, but not even that stopped a tear from escaping.

"But I also knew I was still carrying the same crap inside me that's been there for years, and if there was going to be any chance at all for us, I had to go back and deal with it."

She finally looked at him. "The Deuces?"

"Even before that, I was screwed up. Tara and I—we didn't exactly have a normal upbringing. I told you we moved a lot. About my father's job, but—"

"She told me what it was like," Abby interrupted huskily. "I know how you two would hide with your mother in closets and bedrooms whenever your father thought you were in some kind of danger. Was he really in the CIA? Or was he just suffering from paranoid delusions?"

"He was really with the CIA. And he was really paranoid. The way we grew up?" His eyes darkened. "It was a nightmare. And I'm a lot like him."

She twisted her fingers together. "Paranoid?"

He didn't smile. "Sometimes it seemed that way. But I have a clean bill of mental health."

"So what have you been doing, then?"

"Whatever I needed to do to keep some food in my stomach and a pillow under my head. Construction. Manual labor. Whatever was easy to pick up."

"And easy to leave?"

"I visited Maria's grave. My parents' grave." His gaze was hooded. "Johnny's. He wasn't a good man. But there were days when he was my friend. And I needed to face that."

She couldn't keep up with the tears rolling down her face, and she gave up trying. "You could have told me all this. You didn't have to leave. You didn't have to stay away and never even call!"

"Yeah. I did. Because I needed to realize that I did have a dream. That I'm not so different from my sister after all." He reached out and brushed his thumb over her cheek. "That I wanted this. Home. A life. A front porch." He looked down at Rex, who'd given up on getting his attention and had simply decided to lie across his scuffed biker boot. "A dog."

"He's not up for adoption," she said thickly.

He ignored that. "More importantly, I needed to realize that the only one I could have that with—the only one I wanted, *needed,* to have that with—was you."

She inhaled shakily.

"Love has never come easily for me, Abby. Or with any sort of—" he frowned, searching for the word "—grace," he finally said. "And then one day, there you were. Smiling at me over milk in a crystal glass, and nothing had ever seemed easier. Or more complicated." He touched her hair. His hands were shaking. "You made me laugh again. You gave me peace. And you deserve a lot more than I can ever be."

"Sloan—"

"I want forever." His voice was raw. "And I want it with you. Max has a job for me. A permanent one. So this other guy—"

She caught his face between her hands. "There is no other guy. How could there be? There's only you. There will only ever be you."

His eyes searched hers. "You'll marry me?"

She let out a choked laugh. "Are you asking?"

He reached into his pocket and pulled out a diamond ring that looked delicate and unreal in his long fingers.

"Dillon told me once all I had to do was say *please*," he said huskily. "Yeah. I'm asking. Abby, will you *please* marry me?"

She looked from the ring into his eyes. And she saw forever.

"Yes," she whispered. "Yes, I'll marry you."

"Are you *sure?*"

The diamond winked in the sunlight, and she realized his hands weren't steady. She slowly slipped the ring from his grasp and slid it onto her finger.

It fit perfectly.

"I'm sure."

His lips slowly curved. His eyes lightened. His hands slid behind her, and he slowly pulled her close, lifting her right off her feet until she could feel his heart beating against hers. She pressed her lips to his and twined her arms around him, finally believing that she'd never have to let go. "I've never been more sure of anything in my life," she whispered.

The whoop they heard gave them only a moment's warning before Dillon launched himself at Sloan's legs. "You came back!"

Sloan took a steadying step, managing to set Abby on her feet, though he couldn't bring himself to let her loose. Not completely. Not yet. He hugged Dillon with his other arm, but his eyes never left Abby's beautiful gray ones. "I came *home*."

Her fingers trembled as she stroked his face. She smiled back at him through her tears.

"So are you gonna be Abby's boyfriend *now?*"

"Buddy, I'm going to be a lot more than that," he promised.

Dillon thought about that for a moment. "Guess Grandma's cookies really work."

Sloan threw back his head and laughed. He scooped up Dillon in one arm and pulled Abby against him with his other. "Cookies, huh? So it was really all a plot?"

She lifted her shoulder, blushing almost as bright a red as her shirt. "They didn't work so well for me. It only took my grandmother a month to catch Grandpa. It took me one hundred and forty-six days."

"It's been that many days since I saw your face." He leaned over and kissed her slowly. "But it only took you one day to catch me," he said huskily. "All it took was that smile of yours." The smile he vowed to keep on her pretty face for the rest of his life.

Dillon squirmed and Sloan set him down. Rex immediately jumped against Dillon, and they were off, running around the yard. Sloan wasn't sure who was chasing whom.

Abby slid her arms around his waist and looked up at him. Her eyes were shining. "Welcome home, Sloan." She reached up and pressed her mouth to his.

This was the dream, he knew.

His Abby, who had a heart wide enough to include even a man like him.

* * * * *

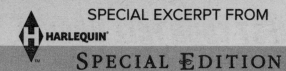
Sutter Traub is a heartbreaker...something Paige Dalton knows only too well. Which is why she's determined to stay as far as she can from her ex! But Rust Creek's prodigal son has come home to help his brother win an election—and to win back the heart of the woman he's never been able to forget...

***

"Sutter?"

He yanked his gaze from her chest. "Yeah?"

She huffed out a breath and drew the lapels closer together. Despite her apparent indignation, the flush in her cheeks and the darkening of those chocolate-colored eyes proved that she was feeling the same awareness that was heating his blood.

"I said there's beer and soda in the fridge, if you want a drink while you're waiting."

"Sorry, I wasn't paying attention," he admitted. "I was thinking about how incredibly beautiful and desirable you are."

She pushed her sodden bangs away from her face. "I'm a complete mess."

"Do you remember when we cut through the woods on the way home from that party at Brooks Smith's house and you slipped on the log bridge?"

She shuddered at the memory. "It wouldn't have been a big deal if I'd fallen into water, but the recent drought had reduced the stream to a trickle, and I ended up covered in muck and leaves."

And when they'd gotten back to the ranch, they'd stripped out of their muddy clothes and washed one another under the warm spray of the shower. Of course, the scrubbing away of dirt had soon turned into something else, and they'd made love until the water turned cold.

"Even then—covered in mud from head to toe—you were beautiful."

"You only said that because you wanted to get me naked."

"Just because I wanted to get you naked doesn't mean it wasn't true. And speaking of naked…"

"I should put some clothes on," Paige said.

"Don't go to any trouble on my account."

***

*We hope you enjoyed this sneak peek
from award-winning author Brenda Harlen's
new Harlequin® Special Edition book,
A MAVERICK UNDER THE MISTLETOE,
the next installment in*
MONTANA MAVERICKS: RUST CREEK COWBOYS.
Available next month.

HARLEQUIN®

SPECIAL EDITION

Life, Love and Family

HOW TO MARRY A PRINCESS

**In the newest addition to her popular miniseries
The Bravo Royales, *USA TODAY* bestselling author
Christine Rimmer introduces readers to a Bravo princess
who will settle for nothing less than true love!**

Tycoon Noah Cordell has a thing for princesses—
specifically, Alice Bravo-Calabretti. He's a man who
knows what he wants, but can he finagle his way
into this free-spirited beauty's heart?

*Available in November
from Harlequin® Special Edition® ,
wherever books are sold.*

HSE65776